The Bridge Between

It did not take either of them long to make the decision. They would marry, despite the old man. They would escape together – to his father's land. He'd long been sick of Linchester, and had sufficient faith in himself as a painter to feel no fears for the future. In the face of Stephen's optimism and Julia's increasing love for him and rebellion against her life at home, the rest was fairly simple. Together they had scraped up the two hundred pounds, married secretly at Linchester Register Office early on an April morning, and directly afterwards the long journey to Cornwall began. During those heady exciting hours Stephen enlarged on his ambition of founding a new group of artists which would not only make his own name famous but establish a completely different trend in modern painting. If Julia had fostered any previous doubts of Stephen's genius, any slight fear that his daring colourful work was not, perhaps, so clever as he believed, they were swept aside by his own self-confidence and the ardour of his eyes as they rested on her.

Mary Williams was born in Leicestershire and educated in Leicester and Wales. She trained as an artist and book illustrator and has written many books for adults; she has also written and illustrated several children's books. She now lives in St Ives, Cornwall.

The Bridge Between

Mary Williams

Woman's Weekly Fiction

A Woman's Weekly Paperback
THE BRIDGE BETWEEN

First published in Great Britain 1992
by Judy Piatkus (Publishers) Ltd
This edition published 1995
by Woman's Weekly
in association with Mandarin Paperbacks
an imprint of Reed Consumer Books Ltd
Michelin House, 81 Fulham Road, London SW3 6RB
and Auckland, Melbourne, Singapore and Toronto

A CIP catalogue record for this title
is available from the British Library
ISBN 1 86056 011 3

Printed and bound by
HarperCollins Manufacturing, Glasgow

Chapter One

On a day in the Spring of 1904 Stephen and Julia Kerr arrived at Port Todric to start their married life in two rooms overlooking the Cornish harbour. They had two hundred pounds between them, two suitcases, painting materials, a hat-box, and a great deal of youthful ambitions. An atmosphere of romance enveloped them as they stepped down from the cab, paid the driver, and with a sense of expectancy and adventure walked up the three steps to the entrance of Number 7, Crab Street. The house was tall, granite-grey with a notice "Rooms TO LET" staring from a window.

They knocked and the door opened to reveal a tall severe-looking woman confronting them. She was dressed all in black, her face was dry and pale, under a high forehead surmounted by a ginger knob of hair. She folded her arms and lifted her chin an inch or two higher.

"Yes?" she said shortly. Julia could feel the shrewd eyes assessing her with a hint of criticism, noting details of the new tightly-waisted blue coat with its froth of white muslin at the neck – the saucy small boater trimmed with pink roses and the reddish-brown "Alexandra fringe" of hair curling towards fly-away eyebrows over the piquant face. Julia swallowed, and to ease the tension pulled her hat-pin free vigorously, shaking her curls. She started to speak but Stephen forestalled her. "We're looking for rooms," he said, "and made enquiries at the station. We were directed here. Our name is Kerr. Stephen Kerr – and this is my wife."

The woman studied them a moment before remarking stiffly, "Glad to hear it, I'm sure. Very particular I am who I take in, being the widow of the late Joseph Tremayne. A pillar of the Chapel he was and would have no funny goings on. Well – " she paused before agreeing in more conciliatory tones " – you'd better come in."

She opened the door wider and stood sentinel-like watching as Stephen heaved the luggage in and they were shown into the front parlour to discuss terms and conditions. The room was spotlessly clean, but musty as though the windows had not been opened for years. Heavy lace curtains and an immense aspidistra in a fancy pot blotted out most of what fading light remained. On one wall hung a text, and opposite it an oleograph in a black frame of a fierce-looking gentleman with a black moustache wearing a black coat buttoned to the neck, and with his hand on a Bible – presumably the late lamented husband.

Mrs Tremayne lit a feeble gas jet, and when the tenancy had been discussed the young couple were shown up a steep narrow staircase to the top of the house where the vacant apartments were divided from the rest of the establishment by a private door. There was also an entrance door at the back opening to steep steps outside.

Julia's first impression on going in was a shock of dismay, the interior appeared so old-fashioned, bleak and depressing in the wan light. But when after a few further admonitions their new landlady had gone, Stephen's optimism reassured her. "It'll look all right tomorrow," he said, with an arm tightly about her shoulders. "You see – it'll be fine for a beginning."

He flung himself on the wiry horsehair sofa. It creaked. "Come on," he said, pulling her down beside him. "It'll be fun."

She laughed then. Like a couple of children they bounced up and down.

"I'll fetch the bags up now," he said, "and don't you dare wear a frown when I get back."

She didn't.

How could she? When Stephen, her new husband, was so happy, and from outside came the nearby pounding of the sea! The future at that moment appeared wonderful. And nothing in the world, she decided, was going to spoil it, ever.

Chapter Two

Julia Benson was just twenty-one when she married Stephen Kerr, and he was twenty-five. The wedding had been a secret affair, for as soon as the friendship had been discovered, Julia, the daughter of a wealthy Midland industrialist living in the suburbs of Linchester, had been forbidden to associate with young Kerr, a mere district librarian's assistant. This did not deter Julia however, who had for long been bored with a secluded conventional existence lived in the company of an irritable elderly father and a vain disinterested stepmother. Tea parties, driving about in the carriage-and-pair, shopping in the city, and the limited chatter of feminine gossip tired her in the extreme. From somewhere she had inherited a restless creative streak which was forever yearning for adventure and a wider scope than was offered to young ladies of her position living in that era.

At her select finishing school in Leamington she had proved to be difficult and disconcerting; and when she returned home, problems had increased between herself and the family. The publication of *Bitter Wind*, her first book written in secret, had exploded like a bomb-shell into that well-ordered household. It was not, according to conventional values, a "nice book", satirising in a fresh naive manner all those things so cherished by the best Edwardian society, and likewise by the Bensons.

Far from appreciating the shrewd creative capacity of his daughter, Richard Benson could only deplore what he termed its vulgarity and lack of taste. The rift had widened between them; Julia, therefore, was the more primed for her romance with Stephen Kerr. Apart from this, there was a great deal about Stephen just then to stir the heart of any young woman. He was not only good-looking, he had that indefinable quality called charm, and an air of "not belonging" to Linchester, which gave to him, in Julia's eyes, an added allure. She learned later that her deductions were partially correct. Though Stephen's mother, a governess, had been born in this district, she'd met on holiday, and later married, a Cornish fisherman who'd been drowned when Stephen was two years old. After this his mother had returned to her family in the Midlands. Three years later she had died, leaving Stephen to be brought up by his uncle, Cam Hopkins, who ran a small drapery store in the suburbs of Linchester. On leaving school the boy was taken into the shop and taught his uncle's trade.

But Stephen never settled. Behind his smile and his charm his ambitions reached to other spheres rather than measuring and cutting material. He had a taste for painting, and his work at the store was neglected in favour of stolen moments with a drawing block and brush. It soon became apparent that young Stephen Kerr was becoming a liability instead of a help to his uncle, and when the chance came to assist at the local library for a modest salary on a rising scale, Stephen grasped it, to the relief of all concerned. This work interested him more. He had found the variety of books stimulating, reading avidly every volume on art he could lay his hands on, and also made time to study twice a week in the evenings at the local art school, where he quickly discovered a certain daring if unconventional aptitude with his brush.

When Julia first started her frequent visits to the library, Stephen had been there for two years. Quite soon they were taking every opportunity of discussing books and ideas together. From the first Stephen had been attracted by the young woman with the pointed chin and red-brown hair, who despite her small stature walked so decisively and with such dignity through the swing doors into the library. She had definite taste in literature. Love tales did not interest her very much; she never enquired for Mrs Henry Wood, as so many girls of her age did, and this interested him. No, her taste was for Ibsen and Strindberg, and Russian writers including

4

Tolstoy and Dostoievsky. When, six months following their first meeting, *Bitter Wind* was published, Stephen's passion leaped to fever pitch. This was no ordinary girl of mere good looks and education, but a personality to be reckoned with. He knew then that he desired and meant to have her, that he would never be at peace until her sweet stubborn lips were willing and eager under his, and she belonged to him completely.

It did not take either of them long to make the decision. They would marry, despite the old man. They would escape together – to his father's land. He'd long been sick of Linchester, and had sufficient faith in himself as a painter to feel no fears for the future. In the face of Stephen's optimism and Julia's increasing love for him and rebellion against her life at home, the rest was fairly simple. Together they had scraped up the two hundred pounds, married secretly at Linchester Register Office early on an April morning, and directly afterwards the long journey to Cornwall began. During those heady exciting hours Stephen enlarged on his ambition of founding a new group of artists which would not only make his own name famous but establish a completely different trend in modern painting. If Julia had fostered any previous doubts of Stephen's genius, any slight fear that his daring colourful work was not, perhaps, so clever as he believed, they were swept aside by his own self-confidence and the ardour of his eyes as they rested on her.

"Of course, we shall have to begin in a small way at first," he said. "I don't see why we shouldn't manage to live on two pounds a week – there are lots of wealthy people down there now. Sure you don't mind being poor for a bit, Julia?"

She took his arm. "Of course not. I don't mind anything if I'm with you. And I'm sure to find a *little* time to do some writing."

"Certainly you will. Everything lies before us."

It all sounded so simple. Sitting close against Stephen in the train, Julia let herself believe that such things as cooking, mending, cleaning, and caring for a man would automatically fill only a portion of the day, leaving the rest free for her own work. Even in the first thrill of her love for Stephen, she could not entirely contemplate giving it up. Neither did she complicate matters by delving into the complexities of her own temperament; and if anyone had said to her, as years later she was to say to one of her own grandchildren:

"You have a demon of creativeness in you which will always be free and belong to no man, and unless you can bring it into line with your own life it will fight you and make war wherever you are", she would have tossed the words aside with amusement and contempt, so convinced she was of the ideal basis of her union with Stephen.

Chapter Three

Julia woke late the next morning, feeling in her limbs and being a languorous tiredness which brought a flush to her cheeks when she remembered Stephen's ardours of the night. She opened her eyes and saw through the door her husband's figure dimly outlined in the other room by the gas ring. There was the clatter of cups on a tray. A little secret smile touched her lips. Then she stretched her arms above her head, yawned, and called softly, "Stephen?"

"Yes, darling?" He came over to her.

"What time is it?"

"Late. Nine-thirty."

"Oh, darling! And generally I'm so good in the mornings – it's one of my virtues, getting up early."

He brought her a cup of tea. "Don't worry, I shan't do this every day. This is a unique occasion."

He kissed her, and after they had drunk the tea they got up and had a makeshift breakfast from the sandwiches left over from the night before. Later they dressed, and in the cold light of day examined the rooms. They really were appalling: the bedroom with its ugly brass bedstead and straw mats on the floor, the hideous mahogany wardrobe which took up half the space, the ugly brown curtains looped with pink ribbon, and the queer smell of soap and mothballs everywhere. In the living room the sofa with the horsehair stuffing pushing out at one side, the awful pictures and peeling chocolate-coloured paint.

"Anyhow," said Julia optimistically, "it smells clean."

"Oh, it has possibilities," Stephen agreed. "After all, we've a table to eat from, and chairs to sit on. What do you say to taking the pictures down?"

Julia was doubtful. "*She* may object."

"We're paying rent, aren't we?" said Stephen. "We ought to be able to do what we like in our own place."

So he stood on a chair and took down the offending prints. Unfortunately two vivid squares of yellow ochre paper confronted them reproachfully from the sickly faded hue of the walls.

"That settles it," said Stephen. "I'll put up my own."

Without more ado he unfastened his bag and presently produced two vivid unframed paintings – one an oil of apples and pears with a picture in the background done in a Van Gogh-ish manner, the other a landscape reminiscent of Cèzanne, but rather more startling.

"There," he said, holding up first one then the other, "these'll brighten things up a bit."

Julia did not quite know what to say. "But they're not framed, how will you fix them?"

"Pin them, of course. One wall's wood."

He produced a box of drawing pins, and in the space of a few moments had the paintings up. He was pleased with the result.

"That's better. Of course, the effect's a bit odd yet, because it's only a starting point. We've got to change the rest now."

"But how are we going to do that? After all, the furniture's as it is. We can't alter that."

"Haven't you got a shawl or anything to put over the sofa?"

"My Paisley one that was Grandma's, yes. But it's to wear, Stephen, it's too good to sit on."

"Let's try it, just to see."

So Julia went to her case, and after a good deal of rummaging produced the shawl, which when spread over the couch did have a brightening effect, and so cheered Stephen that she did not have the heart to remove it.

"And I shall get some paint," he went on presently, "green, I think, apple green, or perhaps royal blue, and re-do the whole room."

"But Mrs Tremayne. Oughtn't we to mention it first?"

He gave one of his oddly disarming grins. "No, my darling,

do it first and show her afterwards. That's always the best way."

As time went by Julia was to realise more and more that this indeed was a characteristic of Stephen's – to act quickly, on the assumption that what he did would be approved of. If not it was a pity, but the thing was done and there you were!

They were unpacking and re-arranging until twelve o'clock. Then Stephen suddenly said he was hungry, and they must have a meal.

"Well, Stephen dear," Julia said sweetly, "I've nothing to cook yet, so perhaps we'd better go out, as it's the first day. And I must drop a note to my father just to say we're all right."

"If you must," her husband agreed. "Very well, we'll have a walk round and find a post office and a cafe somewhere, or perhaps a pub."

"Nice."

Julia squeezed his arm, and a little thrill ran through her. A pub! Why, the family would have a thousand fits – Julia Benson in a pub. Still, she was no longer Julia Benson but Mrs Stephen Kerr. A flood of warmth ran through her. She turned and flung her arms quickly round her husband's neck.

"Oh, Stephen, I do love you."

"And I you," he answered softly, resuming after a moment in a more businesslike tone, "Of course, we won't be able to lunch out other days – not on our budget."

"I know that. You needn't worry. I *can* cook. Even my stepmother admitted that my queen-cakes beat Cook's any day. And I'm good at pastry too."

That pastry-making with an oil stove might be an entirely different matter to pastry-making at Linchester did not occur to either of them as they envisaged their rosy domestic future. Presently they were ready to go out: Julia in a short tightly-belted woollen jacket over a long plum-coloured blouse and skirt, with a large fly-away straw hat perched above her fringe from which hung a veil; Stephen wearing a check cap, belted sports coat, and the fashionable knee breeches with woollen stockings.

They both felt slightly self-conscious, and very much in love with life and each other as they walked down Crab Street arm

9

in arm to the harbour. A few visitors were already lazing in the sunshine, and some fishermen were mending nets on the rocks. The little boats still bobbed peacefully on the surface of the water, their sails dark against the sun. There was a salty tang of fish and weed in the air. A queer excitement seized Julia, an emotion that quickened her heart and brought her footsteps temporarily to a standstill. It was as if, in one swift moment, knowledge of the place – its secret unknown life and its kinship with her, all that it was to be to her, in the future – took possession of her, and she knew with certainty that she had come to stay. Just for a moment her consciousness of Stephen faded into something immeasurably bigger, of which they both were but a part. For that brief second she seemed to glimpse against the background of humped cottages and cliffs her life in its entirety – as a child in the garden at Linchester, and ahead into the years when she was very old. It was an odd feeling.

She must have shivered slightly for Stephen said, "What's the matter, Julia? Are you cold?"

She jerked herself back into the present and laughed softly. "No, I was daydreaming. I *love* this place. I'm going to be happy here."

"Of course you are. I say! The Jolly Admiral! Let's go in, shall we?"

They went through the door of a very ancient-looking inn with a signboard creaking outside on which was painted the grotesque dancing figure of a seafaring man against a background of hills and sea. A number of people, fishermen and artists, were crowded about the passage and in the bar-room to the left. There was a general look of surprise when the couple asked for a meal, and the barmaid – or rather woman, for she was Mrs Gertie Rouse, the proprietress, and quite a character with her high-piled hair and earrings – shook her head with a smile.

"Sorry, my love, no time for meal-making here, though if you want a bite of cheese now . . ."

"You might try The Dragon," another voice suggested from the back.

Gertie frowned. "There's plenty of good bread and cheese here," she stated.

10

"Very well, then, that'll be grand," Stephen agreed. "What do you say, Julia?"

"Yes, of course."

"And beer," he said. "We'll have beer."

"Oh, but – "

"But what?" Stephen said, as they sat down at a small table near the fireplace.

"I've never had *beer* in my life," Julia whispered. Stephen was amused.

"First time for everything," he remarked, with a knowing wink.

A slight flush crossed Julia's face. It occurred to her that there were some things worth learning, and some not. However, the hint of criticism in her mind was only momentary, and as quickly died, leaving her entirely enthralled by the exciting low-ceilinged room with its seaman's chest in one corner, two ships in bottles on the mantelshelf, and the huge oleograph of the Battle of Trafalgar on the wall facing her. A pungent smell of malt and smoke hung thick in the dim light wrapping herself and the crowded company in a rich sleepy intimacy.

The general impression in her mind was a confusion of warmth and many faces. But a few stood out, including a slight man with bright eyes and a pointed goatee beard, chatting to a fisherman with his cap pulled down above a powerful hooked nose and jutting chin, and a large florid dark-haired woman wearing a puce-coloured cape and picture hat. She was standing at the bar with a glass of bitter in her hand, drinking with the rest of them. She was good-looking in a stout middle-aged way; but something about her, a certain overbearing vitality, both fascinated and repelled Julia.

At the moment Stephen noticed her the woman was telling a bawdy story with much gusto, laughing in a loud voice holding the gruff quality of a man's. Stephen smiled at Julia, then quite quickly she saw something else leap into his eyes, something akin to interest, speculation.

"My dear Countess," the little man with the goatee beard was saying, "my dear Countess . . ."

Stephen turned to a man standing near and enquired, "Who is she?"

11

"That? Oh, that's the Countess Lapont. Flamboyant old bird. Quite a character."

"An artist?"

"Well – interested, and got the cash to throw around. Widow of some foreign Count or other."

Stephen nodded, drawing in his breath. "I see."

Later, when they were walking back along the harbour, he said to Julia, "My sweet, I'll have to look in again as soon as possible at the Jolly Admiral."

"Why?"

"Because, my darling, I have decided that the Countess shall be one of my first pupils."

Julia laughed. "You're absurd, Stephen. She may paint already, she may not be a bit interested in your method, or have any idea of being anyone's pupil."

"Then I will make her interested in *us*, Julia. She may be useful."

"Well," said his wife a little tartly, "I don't particularly want her interest, and she wouldn't like me anyhow."

"I'm sure she'll like me though," Stephen assured her blithely, "you just watch."

"I'm sure I shan't," Julia said, "I shall have other things to do."

He squeezed her arm.

"Darling, darling! You're never jealous of that portly old tart? Oh, darling, you are too funny."

"Don't be silly. Jealous of her! And, anyway, you've no right to call her a tart," Julia said primly. Then suddenly she relaxed, smiled, and added sweetly, "I'll be nice to anyone you want me to be, so long as it helps you."

"After all," he said, "influence counts, and if I'm ambitious it's because of you."

"Dear Stephen!"

The momentary irritation had gone. They were once more entirely absorbed in one another, and with his arm round her, made their way to locate the post-office, then back along Crab Street to number seven.

Chapter Four

The next few days were spent by Stephen in re-painting the rooms and titivating the furniture while Julia kept watch and at the first signs of Mrs Tremayne's approach gave warning to her husband. On one pretext or another they managed to keep the unwanted visitor away. On the fourth day they both decided that their ingenuity in this respect was almost exhausted; for Julia, on her way out to shop, was confronted suddenly by the landlady who bobbed out of her own doorway to say formidably, with arms folded: "Good morning! Tell your husband, if you please, Mrs Kerr, that I shall be up this morning, about twelve, to see if the gas meter's in order. And no excuses, mind. The gas meter I *will* see."

"Certainly," Julia answered. "But is there anything wrong? I mean – the meter works, doesn't it?"

"That's neither here nor there!" Mrs Tremayne stated stubbornly, "I'm coming up, and that's final."

"I'll tell him, of course."

"Very well. Twelve o'clock."

Mrs T – as they had both nicknamed her – pursed her lips, inclined her head rather in the manner of a queen conferring a favour, and withdrew, leaving Julia to hurry away fearing a second onslaught.

It was still quite early but the harbour was astir with activity. Seaweed carts were already out, their shapes dark against the pale sands; at the corner of Crab Street the gulls were squawking in a feathered mass where surplus fish was being sorted and sold. Julia approached with her basket. It occurred to her that her husband might be getting a little tired of fish, but at the moment fried meals seemed the only possibility owing to the cooking arrangements and the fact that Stephen's paint tins and brushes were stacked on the limited table space. Looking into her purse she discovered that she had only seven shillings out of the fifteen that was to be her weekly allowance for food. The disclosure was a shock, but also a challenge. It would be simpler later on, she thought, and anyway at the beginning they would have to spend a little more on getting supplies in. When she explained Stephen would understand, and if he didn't she would have to draw on the odd spare pound or two she had brought with her. So she bought some herrings and a small plaice. Then, remembering that vinegar and pepper were needed, also potatoes, she made her way along Salutation Street to the shops.

As she hurried along the narrow road in the spring sunshine, her high-heeled shoes made a light clippety-clop sound on the cobbles, and a rush of wind blew her skirts wildly round her legs. Clutching her hat to her head, she dived into a grocer's. When she'd bought what she needed she recklessly spent another sixpence on a bunch of violets, which she pinned to her coat before making her way back.

On arriving at number seven it was already eleven-thirty, and she noticed that Mrs T's front steps had been newly scrubbed. Julia hurried up to Stephen and informed him of the gas meter dialogue.

"This time she'll *come!*" she told him emphatically. "She suspects something, Stephen, and wild horses won't keep her away."

"Well, what of it?" he replied cheerfully. "She'll hardly recognise the old place."

"I know, that's just it!" Julia agreed anxiously. "It's – it's so *very* different."

"And thank God for that! You're not going to tell me we've not improved it."

Looking round at the blue paint, Stephen's pictures, the varnished chairs, the covered sofa, and the hundred and one other changes which had taken place since their arrival, Julia had to admit it was brighter.

"But she won't like it," she said, "I'm sure of it."

Stephen thought quickly. "Tell you what," he said, after a moment, "we'll go down now and ask her up."

"*Ask* her?"

He nodded. "You've married a man of brains, my dear. What about this?" He went into the bedroom, returning with a bottle of gin.

Julia stared. "But Stephen!"

"Don't say I don't think of things," he grinned. "After a nip of this, Mrs T will be seeing only pink angels in a rosy glow."

Julia giggled. "How funny! But, darling, I don't suppose for a moment she drinks. Methodists don't, you know. Not Cornish ones, anyhow."

"Only at funerals, weddings, and celebrations," Stephen said blithely. "And this *is* a celebration. Come on, Julia, straighten your hair, and let's get down there before she comes up."

She obediently combed her fringe, and a moment later was hurrying down after him.

They found Mrs Tremayne already at her door. Stephen asked if they could speak to her a moment, and giving her no chance to refuse, pushed Julia ahead of him.

Mrs T exclaimed, "Well!" and was about to say more when Stephen brandished the bottle in front of her nose, temporarily silencing her.

"We want you to come and see the rooms now, please, Mrs Tremayne," he said, mustering all the charm he knew. "But first of all we thought perhaps you'd drink our health – my wife's and mine? You see, we've only been married three days. And it's pretty strange down here, knowing no one – no friends, you know, or well-wishers. Except yourself."

They waited expectantly. Julia's heart quickened. Later she said to Stephen, "I thought she was going to pounce on me, her mouth went so tight and funny." And indeed, Mrs T's words were not at first encouraging.

"That stuff!" she said, eyeing the bottle. "And what made you think I'd touch *liquor*, Mr Kerr?"

"I didn't think so for a moment, in the ordinary way," he said, smiling. "But after all . . ." he paused with his brows raised questioningly. And then, with relief, they both saw the landlady's mouth relax slightly, and a certain anticipatory gleam creep into her eyes as she regarded the bottle.

"Well, of course, it makes a difference, I agree – with a wedding to celebrate. But I must impress upon you – tedn't my way at all, touching liquor, Mr Kerr. My husband Jonah was as sound a Methodist and Temperance man as could be found."

"Of course, of course," agreed Stephen, "we realise that. And if you really don't feel you can drink our health, well – "

This was a shrewd touch.

"I didn't say I wouldn't now," she said, "and since you'd take it amiss if I refused, you being my tenants and everything, well – just this once, I suppose."

Stephen gave Julia a dig as they followed the prim figure into her sitting room or 'parlour' as she called it.

Mrs Tremayne told them to sit down, which they both did, side by side on the red plush sofa. Then she went to the cabinet and produced the glasses. They were rather large tumblers for gin, but this suited Stephen, who half-filled Mrs T's for her.

"There, Mrs Tremayne, that couldn't hurt a child."

After the first few sips the grim features relaxed, and their landlady was soon recounting with relish full details of her husband's lovely funeral, and the manner in which his coffin had been carried by bearers for a mile up the hill to Trevathon Church.

"Handsome it was, my dears, handsome,' she said reminiscently, wiping a tear away.

"I'm sure it was," Stephen agreed seriously.

"They don't have funerals like that these days," Mrs T concluded with satisfaction.

Feeling an irresistible desire to smile, Julia smothered her weakness behind a simulated sneeze. Really, she thought, Stephen should have been an actor; it was amazing the way he kept himself under control and managed to flatter and profess interest at the same time. Anyone might have thought him an undertaker, so well versed in the ways of funerals he seemed.

Ten minutes went by, at the end of which Mrs Tremayne appeared to have lost all recollection of the gas meter. Stephen reminded her gently, at which she rose to her feet with unsteady amiability.

"Of course," she said, with an effort at dignity. "We'll go up now."

She smiled, swayed a little, and pressed her hand to her forehead.

"Allow me," said Stephen, offering her his arm.

And so, with the forced deliberation of one who knows herself to be slightly inebriated, Mrs T marched with Stephen from the parlour up the stairs to the flat.

The rest of the meeting went cheerfully and according to plan. Mrs Tremayne, wrapped in the rosy glow of Stephen's gin, approved the alterations, and the end of the little interlude resulted in her signing a written appreciation of all the young Kerrs had done – this compiled by Stephen – together with her consent to a three-monthly tenancy instead of one.

Stephen's adroitness gave Julia a strange momentary feeling of being apart from him. He was clever, and of course she loved and admired him tremendously; she would never get over the thrill of being in his physical presence. But something cold and clear-sighted in her – something of the same ruthless conscience which was her father's – argued that maybe he was a little *too* clever. After all, there were ways of doing things. It would somehow have been nicer if they had got their agreement with Mrs T through different means.

When the landlady had gone, a vestige of this must have shown in Julia's manner, but Stephen laughed at her, and with his usual charm soon jerked her out of her mood.

"You've got a conscience!" he mocked lightly. "You don't think I've been quite nice! Oh, but Julia – I've done it all for you. Besides, my dear, we've improved her property no end. *She* ought to be the grateful one!"

Julia accepted the assurance with relief. Really, how wrong it was of her to criticise Stephen! And what he said was perfectly correct. But though she tossed the matter aside she recognised deep in her heart that passionately as they loved each other, Stephen and herself saw differently on some things, and would never share the same intrinsic values. The knowledge came as a shock.

That same week, however, any lingering doubts were swept from her mind by a note she received from her father.

17

The letter, written on the family notepaper headed Crich End, Linchester, read:

My dear Julia,

To say that I was grieved and upset by your selfishness and lack of consideration will be no news to you, for whatever your faults you are no fool and cannot therefore expect me to accept your actions with anything but pain – pain that a daughter of mine could so wilfully and consciously have deceived me during the past months. I am not going to qualify my statements further, since you have apparently lost all sense of obligation and affection to me.

You were always headstrong, Julia, and have now made it quite clear that you prefer to blunder your own way through unfavourable circumstances rather than accept with any sense of gratitude the comforts and advantages of a good home. From this moment, therefore, I shall treat you no longer as a child of mine. While your life is linked to Stephen Kerr's your allowance ceases completely, and you may expect no help from me whatever. This is final. And if that upstart good-for-nothing husband of yours thinks to get a penny out of me, you can tell him he is grossly mistaken.

I remain,
Your disappointed father,
Richard Benson

After reading the letter, Julia sat for some moments with the scrap of paper tightly folded in her hands. Her colour paled then deepened, bringing two brilliant spots of red to her high cheek bones. Her first reaction was one of outrage on Stephen's behalf. How dare her father speak of him like that? Stephen, who was so charming and clever, and had been content to marry her with nothing at all? Then, slowly, indignation gave place to a stubborn acceptance. After all, it was better that way. It was what she should have expected, and both she and Stephen had talent and brains. *Bitter Wind* had been written in defiance, under frustrating circumstances.

How much stronger and richer her next book would be, with Stephen's love and understanding for support.

Just then he put out his hand.

"Your father?" he said.

She nodded.

"Let me see."

"I'd rather not."

"I have a right to know how things stand," he insisted.

She handed him the note, watched his face pale and the sudden tightening of the jaw. Then he threw the letter on the table, laughed, and lit a cigarette.

"Who cares?" he said lightly, contemptuously.

"Well, if *you* don't . . ."

"I?" He took her into his arms. "Your father thinks me a fortune hunter, my darling, but I can assure you I wouldn't touch a penny of his with a barge pole. I didn't marry you because you were Richard Benson's daughter, but because I loved you."

He kissed her again and again.

"There! Does that satisfy you?"

"Oh, yes, Stephen, of course. Of course – I *know*."

"But it just shows," he went on practically, "we must get going. I must see about a studio tomorrow, have a look round. Perhaps it'll be possible to pick up something cheap. I was speaking to an old fisherman fellow last night who might let me have an attic where he keeps his nets. And I must look in at the Jolly Admiral. Contact with people matters, you know."

Julia knew he was thinking of the Countess, and was not surprised later that evening when he suggested going out for a drink.

"I shan't be long, darling," he promised her. "Come with me if you like, of course, but – "

"Oh, no," Julia said, slightly hurt. "No, I won't. You'll feel freer on your own anyway. And I don't much like the Countess woman."

He smiled. "As you choose. I shall soon be back."

"I'll get some more of my things packed away," she told him. "Oh, and by the way, we didn't budget for laundry or washing. I won't be able to afford *that* out of the fifteen shillings."

19

"Laundry?" Stephen looked blank. "Good Lord!" I'd forgotten that. Anyhow, what's it matter now? We can talk about it later."

"I suppose I could do it myself," said Julia, not entirely meaning this and expecting a sharp denial. To her astonishment he agreed.

"Well, there won't be much, of course. We could get a large bowl, and fix a line somewhere."

"Yes, why not?"

She spoke lightly, though with a sinking feeling at heart. Cleaning, cooking, washing-up – and now on top of it Stephen's shirts and collars to iron, his socks to darn. Of course it was all a part of marriage – it was what thousands of women did year in and year out, and she had known they would be poor. But Stephen was particular about his clothes! And it was not as if she had been used to it.

For a second she felt a spasm of gloom. It was growing darker outside, and the gas was not yet lit in the living room. She no longer had a father to whom she could run and say: "Please, I want a little money." It was a funny feeling, this being alone with Stephen in a world which allowed only fifteen shillings a week for living on.

On an impulse she ran to her husband and clung to him, her arms around his neck.

"You *do* love me, Stephen, don't you?" she asked urgently, like a child demanding reassurance.

He smiled and pulled her close to him. "What a question! Love you? I could devour you."

He kissed her hotly. But it was not the answer she had hoped for. She withdrew gently, striving for dignity.

"And now," she said, "perhaps you'd better go – if you want to catch the Countess."

He looked slightly puzzled. "Sure you don't mind?"

"Quite sure."

A few moments later he was gone, and Julia was left in number seven confused, disappointed, with a queer inexplicable sensation of loneliness about her. Yet why was that? What had Stephen done, or not done, that could account for it? Life was odd. A short hour or so ago and they had been as one, without a care in the world. Now, for no apparent cause whatever, they were somehow two people, a little apart from each other, living and acting in their own separate worlds. Tonight, of course, it would be different again! Tonight she would lie in Stephen's arms, and physical contact would once more unify them. Meanwhile she must not brood, there was so much to do. Looking round the room, she sighed. Yes, indeed, there was still a very great deal to be got through before number seven had really become a home.

Chapter Five

The next few weeks brought many revelations to the young Kerrs. Both Julia and Stephen – loving each other passionately – had quick tempers, and there were times when Julia's, frayed by the complications of life on a meagre allowance and under difficult circumstances, flared into rebellion. Though she tried to stifle it, resentment of Stephen's absences from her gnawed at her angrily when she was left alone too long in the small living room waiting for his return, her ingeniously cooked meal spoiling on top of the inadequate stove.

She knew that his work and their future necessitated these 'social contacts' of his, but she knew also that Stephen was pleased for it to be so, and consequently found it hard to suppress bitter words when he returned merrily half an hour or an hour late, smiling like a boy, full of plans and enthusiasm. Sometimes she gave way to annoyance, and in time Stephen was quick to answer back, so that before they knew where they were, they were in the throes of a quarrel. Afterwards, at night, it was always right – they made it up and Julia promised herself and Stephen that she would try to be more reasonable, although it occurred to her sometimes that it was always she who had to do the apologising, like a child who must of necessity be in the wrong. But this, she thought, in the sweetness of reconciliation, was probably as it should be; in any case such details were not important in the face of their love for each other.

So for a time their happiness was as great as ever, until some new cause arose at which the hidden doubt, the financial insecurity of their life together, was quick to ignite like a flame in her mind. She was not, she found, at all the kind of person she had thought herself to be in the days before her marriage. There were ugly strange roots of jealousy and possessiveness in her which with her better nature she despised and abhorred.

Perhaps if Stephen had understood, or even tried to, they would never have flowered above the surface. But Stephen did not understand. It was incomprehensible to him that a girl whose sensitivity so pleased him in *Bitter Wind* could under provocation appear shrewish and harsh.

"I'm not *really* like that," she said to him more than once, "really I'm not. It's just – "

"Then why do you do it?" he said desperately. "*Why*?"

Julia looked at him dumbly. He was really puzzled and hurt. That was the whole trouble; he just didn't *see* – didn't realise what a change it all was – the washing and rubbing till her knuckles were sore, the fetching of water, and constant cooking and washing-up, the endless difficulties of the household arrangements which confronted her while Stephen was discussing art in studios and bars, away from her. He *didn't* understand; Stephen was no psychologist, so he probably never would. Always, on these occasions, Julia searched wildly for a solution, for some means which would unify their existence and bring back her natural equilibrium. It was not easy. But to outweigh the bad times there were the good when they had fun and were like children together, or lovers caught up once more in the first ecstasies of passion. Then it seemed that the rest was a bad dream, and nothing mattered but that they were married and together.

On a day in May Stephen came back in the afternoon to tell Julia that he had not only found a studio but that they had been invited to an evening at the Countess's.

"It's all working out as I intended," he said glibly and gaily. "You must look your very best, my sweet. There'll be people there. It may mean something."

"And I'm expected to amuse them, I suppose?" she said tartly, recollecting the florid charms of the Countess.

Stephen stared at her. "*Darling*!"

"Oh, I'm sorry," she said, swiftly repentant, "truly I am.

But I've had such an afternoon – you've no idea. First the stove went wrong, then it flared and there were black things everywhere. Then that awful cat from next door knocked the milk jug over and broke it, and on top of everything I cut my finger. Look!" She paused, breathless, holding out her bandaged first finger.

"What a shame," he was genuinely solicitous. "Is it bad?"

Shaking her head she admitted honestly. "No, not really."

He laughed. "Cheer up, darling, we'll have a jolly evening tonight, and you'll enjoy it."

"Shall I? Well, I hope so," Julia said doubtfully.

"You must put your best on," her husband resumed. "The lilac velvet, with the waist and no shoulders."

"The *evening* one?" gasped Julia. "But, Stephen, it's so – well, it's not the kind of dress for an informal affair. I've only worn it once."

"And the more reason why you should wear it tonight," he insisted. "You've got to startle them, Julia."

"But why? If I was the only one dressed up it would be awful. Don't you see?"

"No, I don't. You can put on the earrings with it, the crystal ones."

"I certainly shan't wear those," his wife said sharply, "whatever you say, Stephen, and that's that."

Recognising the danger signals Stephen let the matter of the earrings drop, sensing that he had at least won his point concerning the dress, over which later events proved him to be right. For had Julia worn the skirt and blouse which she'd intended to, she'd have felt considerably out of place in the bizarre scene confronting them three hours' later. The Countess's studio, furnished luxuriously in a haphazard style with numerous Persian rugs, pieces of Indian drapery, French ornaments and a mixture of antique pieces, was hardly a fitting background for tailor-mades. Neither was the company which, apart from their hostess, included one or two long-haired young men, and a very pale, very beautiful young woman, wearing a sea-green frock over which she had draped a multi-coloured Paisley shawl.

Stephen and Julia were greeted effusively. The Countess was outrageously attired in a pair of yellow silk trousers with a loose kimono jacket, and was smoking a cheroot from an amber holder. Earrings dangled below her black curled hair, and she was liberally rouged.

What a dreadful woman! Julia thought, with a stab of dismay. She must be copying Georges Sand.

But Stephen, apparently, was far from thinking so. He smiled and gently kissed his hostess's hand, while Julia's lips tightened into a frozen line. How *could* he! It was humiliating – to behave like that to a woman he hardly knew. Then she became aware that Stephen was nudging her, and that the Countess was speaking to her.

"My *dear!* So you are the little wife of this clever young man? How delightful. Stephen, my dear, she is quite charming. And I hear you write little stories too – "

"I write," said Julia, shortly and sweetly, dangerously sweetly, "but my stories are neither little nor very nice. You probably wouldn't like them, Countess."

There was a general titter, and one of the long-haired young men murmured, "Witty – oh, very witty," in a bored drawl.

"Oh, call me Annette," the Countess said to Julia. "Everyone I like calls me Annette. And I like everyone except fools, and you're certainly not that. So sit down and be sociable."

Julia sat on the divan next to one of the young men who was introduced to her as Manfred Moulin. He wore a huge bow and rosette in his buttonhole, reminiscent of the *Yellow Book* and Aubrey Beardsley.

Stephen was given a pouffe on which he ensconced himself near the Countess and the beautiful young woman.

"Amuse Andrea while I get the drinks," the Countess told him. "She's a protégé of mine, and you'll find her interesting. She portrays people from a completely new angle – not what they look like, but what they *are*. A really naughty mind, although you wouldn't think it, would you, with her looks? But she's had two husbands already, let me warn you."

The Countess flashed a look and winked at Julia.

"Don't worry, darling, he's quite safe. Andrea's absorbed in her art."

Julia flushed. She disliked the party and was already wondering how long it would have to be before she could suggest

25

to Stephen, without giving offence, that it was time to go. A moment later the Countess brought a tray across with drinks already poured.

"Take what you fancy," she said, "whisky, gin, or my special concoction. A 'blue demon' I call it – gin with a nip of sherry and the rest!"

Julia helplessly glanced at Stephen who threw her a mischievous grin before leaving her to the mercies of the Countess.

"Oh, don't be 'pie', dear," she insisted. "Try a blue demon."

"I'm not used to spirits," Julia answered, "so perhaps – "

"Always a first time," the obnoxious voice persisted with a trill of laughter. "Named after a favourite filly my husband – my *first* husband – gave me. A great judge of horses Hiram was – horses and money. Not like the Count, bless him, who couldn't tell a mare from a stallion. Up in the air *he* was – poetry and art. Funny he liked me. But he did, by God! 'You make me laugh, Annie,' he'd say. 'Mon dieu, but you make me laugh!'"

Julia took the glass helplessly, and the Countess pinched her cheek.

"You'll get used to me in time, my dear. Don't mean half I say. But I know life and I know men. Keep 'em amused. Annie Potts – that's me, my dear – learned that in the front row of 'Dick Benson's Girls' thirty years ago."

Discomforted and disgusted, Julia sipped from the glass. Minutes later her revulsion was giving place to a bored defiance which was not entirely unpleasant. She saw Stephen opposite her looking slightly unreal, staring into the eyes of the beautiful maiden. By then the Countess had her arm round his shoulders.

Julia felt the colour flame into her cheeks in a wave of anger.

"Stephen!" she cried, rising to her feet.

"Well?" he said lazily, totally uninterested. His wife sighed, flopped back into a chair, and found the young man next to her refilling her glass.

"No! No thanks," she said abruptly.

"Oh, but I say, you *must*. One really can't be exclusive at a party."

The rest of the evening became something of a nightmare to Julia. She was aware at one point of a young man reading a confused poem about sex and souls which he'd written himself, and that Stephen and the Countess were engaged in some discussion of art. The atmosphere became a seething whirl of libidos, love and self-expression, and through the blurred medly of voices she heard the Countess insisting throatily that Stephen had got hold of the "real thing", that together they could revolutionise the art of Port Todric. Beyond the smoke and heat she could see Andrea's long green eyes gleaming with catlike sleepy enthusiasm. The whole room felt to her incredibly evil.

"I'm going, Stephen," she said suddenly, forcing herself to a cold sobriety. "It's late."

She stood up, reaching a little unsteadily for her cape.

Stephen frowned. "Oh, but, look here – "

"I'm *going*," Julia flashed. "Come if you like, or stay. I don't care."

Stephen sought to save the situation, while the Countess smiled and seemed to derive great amusement from it.

"Go, dear," she said soothingly, "your little wife's tired and unstrung. It's new to her, all this. Some other day."

"I'm not at all tired," Julia said with heightened colour. "I just can't stick the heat and – and – "

"And us," the Beardsley young man finished for her. "Oh dear, you're quaint, too quaint."

He lay back again, closing his eyes.

Julia made for the door. Stephen was quickly after her. His eyes were cold, his voice icy as he said, "Very well, if you're not comfortable we'll go."

At the door he apologised for her mood to the Countess.

"Don't worry, dear boy," his hostess said. "There's no need. Lord, I understand! And our little project, remember – we'll meet tomorrow at the Admiral and go into it. I like you, Stephen, you've got guts."

"Guts!" said Julia when they stood outside. "What a crude word! What a really awful party. I'll never go back there again, *never*!"

"You won't get the chance," he said in a cold voice. "I shan't take you. Humiliating me like that."

"*I* humiliated *you*?' exclaimed Julia, aghast. "How *can* you say that?" She was near to tears.

"Well, what else was it?" he persisted. "You know very well I went there for a reason. Yet all you did was to make things impossible and insult the Countess."

"Insult a woman like that?" Julia said contemptuously. "Oh, Stephen."

"The truth is that you're jealous," he went on angrily, "plain jealous."

"Don't be ridiculous," said Julia, her voice rising.

"Be quiet can't you?" Stephen shook her arm.

Julia wrenched herself free. "Let me alone."

"Certainly, if you're sober enough to stand up."

This was really dreadful. Quarrelling in the street like common brawlers! Julia, jerked to herself by the argument, walked on silently, coldly aloof, with Stephen by her side likewise speechless and sullen. The mood had not lifted when they reached number seven. They went up the steps and entered without a word between them. Seen through eyes of despair the little room looked hopelessly tawdry to Julia. When she had taken off her cape she said to Stephen, not looking at him, "Do you want a drink – tea or anything?"

"No thanks," he answered, in a muffled voice. Then he swung round and faced her. At first she thought he was about to apologise or at least offer the olive branch, but a second later she knew her mistake.

"Look here, Julia," he said, "you'd better understand at the beginning that I won't have this sort of thing. Either you behave decently when we're out together, or I go alone. Where my plans are concerned, and my work, I won't have interference. It isn't as if we're independent. We neither of us have any money, so we've got to make the best of our chances. The Countess and people like her are going to make a lot of difference to us. And I'm damn' well not going to stand by and see you mess things up!"

"Indeed?" Julia's voice was icy. "And do you really think that you're going to do anything worthwhile through – through *that* sort of thing and *that* sort of person?"

"Yes, I do. The Countess has money, and we need it. I need

28

it for the school. I'm going to have that school, Julia, however much you may fight against it."

"Against it? But I'm not against it," she said with genuine amazement. "I want it as much as you, but there are ways and ways – "

"Well, I'm going to have it *my* way," he stated with finality. "And if the Countess wants to back me – which she mayn't, after the way you acted tonight – I'll be only too glad. Her money's as good as anyone else's, and she's a good sort anyhow. And a lot more intelligent than you seem to think."

"I really didn't have much chance of appreciating her intelligence," Julia said acidly. "Sorry".

Stephen's eyes narrowed as he stared at her. "Hm! You look a regular shrew, let me tell you, with that expression on your face. If you go on in this way, Julia, you'll be a hag by the time you're forty."

She was suddenly tired. "Stephen – *need* we?" she asked in a softer voice.

He shrugged. "Well, it's up to you."

"But *is* it? All of it?" she asked. "Is it *always* my fault?"

He shook his head. "I don't know." He put his hand to his forehead. "I feel hellish."

"No wonder. All those awful blue demons!"

Despite themselves, they began to smile. But later, as they lay in bed, Stephen said to her following the inevitable reconciliation, "Remember, Julia, I meant it – you mustn't interfere, not with my work."

"Very well, Stephen."

Her voice was meek, but she was thinking: It's *got* to be different. Somehow he must be made to see.

And Stephen's thoughts ran: I'll mould her in time, she's only a child really. It's only a matter of letting her see I'm master in my own house.

"Julia," he murmured, reaching out to her, "I do love you, you know."

She stirred sleepily. "Yes, of course, I know that."

But was that what he wanted her to say? He was not quite sure. Really, women were not easy sometimes.

Chapter Six

The next day Stephen saw the Countess again. She informed him that she already had one or two pupils for him, including the lovely Andrea who, of course, would follow along her own lines of work, but would be a good advertisement for him.

"And of course," she went on, "you'll be able to help her with her colour. Her drawing's good, but colour – she hasn't got the hang of it at all. Too pale."

Stephen was delighted with the interview, and, appearing to have forgotten his argument with Julia of the night before, related it in full detail to his wife when he returned.

Julia was quiet and self-contained. "Good," she said when Stephen told her he was beginning the classes the following week. "It'll be better for you to get started."

"Better for both of us," he said. "The Countess is being very generous really, getting me quite good fees, and having advertisement sheets printed, and all sorts of tackle for me. We're in luck, darling."

And so the school opened the following week, with four pupils who met at nine o'clock on the Monday morning. Julia went down with Stephen at an earlier hour to see that everything was in order. He was excited and enthusiastic as any boy.

"It's got atmosphere already," he declared. And, indeed, the studio had a romantic look in the early light. Beams of pale sunlight filtered through the skylight and windows, glinting across easels, stools, and odds and ends of canvasses, provided mostly by the Countess. A fisherman's net was bundled in one corner, and a few cobwebs still draped the recesses between beams and walls. Julia suggested removing them, but Stephen waved her scruples aside.

"No," he objected, "it's more romantic as it is. Leave them, Julia. In the light they look – well – kind of ghostlike and strange."

She laughed. "But, Stephen, that's not like you a bit! Generally you're so fastidious over things like that."

A faraway look had come into his face. "Yes, but this is different. It would be like disturbing dreams somehow – and I want all my dreams, Julia."

She took his arm. "I like you to talk this way. I never thought . . ."

"Well?"

"Oh, nothing."

"You never thought I had it in me," he finished for her. "You thought all I pondered over was money, and how to make it."

"No, not quite that."

"A man has to think of the practical side," he went on, "but that doesn't mean the other isn't there. Don't you see? My – well – the mercenary streak you seem to find in me, is only proof that I want something terribly badly. The Stephen Kerr School! oh, Julia, think! Years ahead, when we're very old, and after that, this will go on."

"Yes, Stephen," she agreed in a quiet voice, almost humbled by his enthusiasm.

"Something tangible," he resumed, "an idea become concrete, growing year by year. A whole new trend in painting."

Standing there with him the idea no longer seemed so remote to Julia. She saw them as pioneers, forerunners of a completely new art.

How clever he was, and how incredibly dear!

He must have sensed her mood, for he looked down suddenly, and seeing her face transfigured, glowing with excitement and warmth, a rush of love for her surged up in him. He pulled her to him abruptly, kissing her hotly, passionately.

When he released her she stood smiling, breathless and radiant as a child.

31

"Oh, Stephen, it's beginning – it's going to come true."

"Of course it is, and more. Did you doubt it?"

And indeed it seemed at that moment that all was harmony and promise, and no shadow of misunderstanding could ever again come between them. Outside the gulls were crying round the roofs and chimney pots, while the great waves rolled on the beach in a rhythm of force and sound. Like the inevitable pulse of eternity they rose and fell in constant reiteration, to which Julia felt the beat of her own heart respond, strong and certain. As in the first days of their love, she felt creativeness rise in her – a strength that leaped beyond time and space into endless unknown spheres. There was nothing she could not do – nothing! So long as things remained like this, with Stephen and herself in accord. Just for a moment they touched that perfection that comes but rarely in a lifetime, and is impossible to hold.

Then they heard steps on the stairs, and a minute later the door was opened.

The Countess stood there in a loose black cape, with a velvet hat perched floppily and somewhat absurdly on her black curled hair. Seeing Stephen, she smiled and came forward.

"My dear boy, I just had to come! It's too exciting. Imagine it, – the first time for years I've been up before ten-thirty! Forgot to put my corsets on, too, until Lou-Lou reminded me. What I should do without her I don't know. Had her since before I married poor Hiram. My dear – " turning to Julia, " – forgive me. But after all, everyone wears them, don't they? Corsets, I mean! So I'm not *really* so outré. And an occasion like this is too exciting, anyhow, for prudery."

Julia smiled. She could afford to in the face of her newly-established understanding with Stephen.

"Certainly it is," he agreed, with a grin.

"And listen," the Countess went on, "I've been thinking. Yes, I was thinking in my bath last night – you'll have to have a model. I think I've got the very person – a little French waitress at the Black Cockatoo. Doesn't earn much, and got a child to keep. She'd jump at it. No false scruples about nudity and all that. What do you say?"

"Of course. The very thing."

"Mind you, it'll be best to keep quiet about it – the life work, I mean – or you'll likely as not end with a ducking."

"What on earth do you mean?" gasped Stephen.

"The fishermen, dear. They don't like it. Not starky bodies – offends 'em, poor darlings. Hmm! And yet old Tommy Trevorrow was found one night spying through the skylight on Mrs Nichols in her nightie. Not but what she wouldn't be worth spying on, poor thing – thirteen stone at the least. But still . . ."

Stephen laughed. "Inconsistent," he agreed.

"Well, I should call it by another name. But what's the odds? All you've got to remember is to keep quiet with the natives."

A slight frown touched Stephen's brows. "But in time it'll have to go," he insisted. "The prejudice, I mean. After all, art can't be carried on in the dark. Publicity's important."

"Yes, but not *that* sort of publicity – not yet," the Countess went on.

"Well then," Stephen said, "the thing to do is to win their confidence – the natives, I mean. Get friendly with them and make things easy that way."

"If you can do that, dear, you'll have achieved something," the Countess told him. "But, there! *You* may be able to do it. Why not? I've faith in you. And I may be an old fool in some things, but believe me – I know men."

I'll bet you do, Stephen thought. Aloud he said, "I suppose there's no danger of our being stoned on the beach when we're sketching?"

"Not so long as you sketch the right things," the Countess told him. "But don't expect to be popular. Artists aren't, down here."

Although he had sensed this before, the news was disquieting to Stephen, who would have preferred a clean field before him. However, he was too much occupied that day to allow the matter to worry him. The Countess left soon after, followed by Julia, leaving him alone to put the finishing touches to the room before the students arrived.

At five-thirty he was back at Crab Street, full of news and excitement over the day's happenings.

"Two of them aren't bad," he said. "There's a yellow-

33

bearded fellow with a fancy for spooks and skulls, but he's got an imagination, if only he'd give it more kick. Then there's an old dame – Miss Brinsley Barrington. She's simply dreadful – a taste for fairies and spiritualism, with roses in her hat and lace on her bosom. *She* won't stay long. The other fellow – Mark Long – he's *good*. You must meet him. Then Andrea . . ." he paused, frowning slightly.

Julia looked up enquiringly. "Yes?" she prompted.

Stephen shook his head. "I don't know. Can't quite make her out. She can draw brilliantly when she wants to – she might make a name if she could bring herself down to earth. But . . ."

"But what?"

"She's a strange girl."

"Oh? *How* strange? In what way?"

"Remote, somehow. She makes you think of – " He broke off, laughed, and went on after a moment, "I dunno. It's just her eyebrows, I expect."

"Eyebrows? Stephen, what on earth are you talking about?"

"They slant," he said. "They fly away like swallows. And with those amazing green eyes – "

Julia was suddenly businesslike. "Do eat your ham, Stephen," she said, "it'll be getting cold."

But there was a little icy fear at her heart, a chill sense of discomfort which she could neither laugh nor will away. Silly of her, of course. But why, oh why, was there always something – some tiny thing to spoil the even tempo of her thoughts and life with Stephen?

Chapter Seven

In a month the group was more or less organised; none of the members appeared to question Stephen's qualifications or his right as an artist to tutor others, and by the end of August two more students had been enrolled. For a time, carried along by her husband's enthusiasm and success, Julia was happy, forgetting her former misgivings over Andrea, reconciling herself willingly to Stephen's absences from her since he returned always so full of life and glad to be with her again. All that summer the weather was warm, the days windless, filled with sunshine lighting the clear sea to jade and amber and purest pale purple. Julia's days were full with chores and the problem of keeping Mrs T in comparative good temper, leaving her little time for wandering and dreaming along the shore or cliffs. But in the evening sometimes she and Stephen would go for a stroll through the quiet twilight scented with wild flowers and brine. Gulls drifted, beautifully poised on the currents of air, to the island where they nested. Long-liners rested on pale sands before settling out for the night's fishing.

Sometimes Julia would think idly, and a little poignantly, of the hours she had thought to spend with her work. Ideas for stories flashed through her mind, and she would plan for leisure time in which to start. Then, when the next day came, there was always something else of immediate domestic concern needing her attention, and the moment would slip by unfulfilled. So long as they were happy together she did not rebel, accepting it as the price of marriage. Even their periodic visits to the Countess became bearable, and to please Stephen Julia arranged occasional 'get togethers' with drinks and sandwiches for his friends at their flat, although there was generally some reckoning or other with Mrs Tremayne the following day.

Sometimes she thought that Stephen was a little too self-absorbed, took her a little too much for granted. Then she told herself that she was probably being egocentric herself, and pushed the thought aside.

One day he came home looking white and somewhat distraught to tell her that there had been a scene at the studio.

Julia was frying potatoes over the oil-stove. She turned round quickly, rubbing her hands on her apron.

"But, Stephen, what sort of a scene?"

"Yokels," he said, "boors – a handful of natives. Good Lord! I didn't know I should be in for this sort of thing."

He looked worn out.

Julia came over to him. "Darling, what *do* you mean? Tell me, Stephen."

"I recognised some of them," he told her. "Polcurnow the butcher, and Tommy Perryn. Then there was that religious fellow who preaches on the harbour – a lay minister at the chapel there on the cliff. Religion! For two pins he'd have laid me out."

"Stephen, do *explain*!"

"I'm telling you," he said. "They came banging on the door, shouting something – luckily I didn't give them a chance of seeing inside. And what do you think they wanted?"

"I've no idea."

"Marianne, poor kid. You know, the model. Probably put up to it by old Price who runs the Black Cockatoo – didn't like losing cheap labour. But, heavens above, Julia! The names they called her. 'Woman of sin', 'trollop'. And me too – 'dirty furriner' who seduces young women – crying the curses of God upon my head. 'Look here,' I said, 'you've got me all wrong. Marianne's all right, and we're decent people here, so you've no cause for alarm.' But would they listen? Hah! Polcurnow thrust his great fist under my nose, shouting all the abuse under the sun. Long came to my rescue and we managed to lock the door in their faces. Afterwards Trevaskiss – the fisherman I took the studio from – poked his head in. But he was all right, except for his language. Cursed the other lot,

36

who luckily for us belong to a rival chapel, and told me he'd give 'em hell if they set their dirty feet on his premises again. Luckily Marianne was dressed by then, so he couldn't complain of anything *there*. But my word! If they'd got the girl, I wouldn't have been in her shoes for anything."

Julia looked incredulous. "But it sounds so primitive and stupid," she said. "They couldn't do physical violence to a girl just because she posed for a painting?"

"Couldn't they, though! One had a stick, and little Perryn was hugging half a brick. I tell you, Julia, it's given me a shock. However, after two hours or so they seemed to have dispersed. Andrea's offered to keep an eye on Marianne – took her home with her, accompanied by Long and another fellow. I've told her not to turn up tomorrow. Just in case."

"Oh." Julia was solemn. After a moment she asked, "What will you do? Go to the police?"

Stephen shook his head. "Not at present. It would be fatal. When it comes to the point, the local police are generally more kindly disposed to natives. Besides, our name would be mud for ever after if we got local folk into trouble. And they're not *all* trouble makers, you know. Some of the natives are splendid blokes. It's just one or two."

"Well, what *is* going to happen?"

Stephen shook his head wearily. "Don't ask me at present, I don't know. But one thing's certain, Julia – I won't give in. A few fanatics shan't intimidate me in this way. This school's going on, if I have to quell a thousand Cornish."

Hearing his speak, and watching the hardened lines in his face, Julia thought how he had matured since their marriage those few months ago. He no longer looked a boy, but a man of purpose with a ruthless determination about his eyes and mouth.

"It'll all blow over, I expect," she said soothingly. "Now they've seen you mean to go your own way."

"I'm not so sure about that," he said moodily.

Late that evening they had another disturbance. Julia and Stephen were having a pot of tea before going to bed when they heard Mrs Tremayne's voice raised in anger below. Instantly they were on the alert, listening. Stephen went to the door.

37

"It's that fellow – the lay preacher," he whispered to Julia, "the one who made trouble this morning."

"Seems as though he's making more trouble," she giggled.

"Ssh! Don't laugh. He may be on our track again."

For a few minutes the voices became inaudible. Then once again there was a crescendo of sound and the rattle of a door.

"Come here, Julia," Stephen said softly. "Just look."

Below they saw Mrs T's side door open and through it emerge the figure of a small, dark, violent-looking man, followed by that of Mrs Tremayne, who looked equally formidable.

"And you get off my doorstep, Joe Traill," she was shrieking, "or I'll know the reason why. And don't you come here with your dirty tales polluting *my* house. Get back to them heathens and tell 'em Sarah Tremayne's put you in your place. Well, get out! Get *out!*"

Her last words ended in a shriek; at the same moment she brandished a flat-iron wildly after the retreating figure who did not stop for more but slipped quickly into the entry out of sight.

Julia could not help laughing.

"Oh dear! Oh, Stephen – Mrs Tremayne! How ridiculous. Did you ever *see* anything so funny?"

Just then their landlady emerged again and came pounding up the steps to their room. She entered without knocking, and with arms folded on her bosom faced them truculently.

"Well," she said, "the real rights and wrongs of it I'm not knowing, and tedn' my business to go shielding artists. But one thing be sure and certain – I'm not having that hypocrite Joe Traill fouling my tenants or me. No. Mind you, don't you go thinking I approve of all your goings on, young man, because I don't, and that's that. But *him! That* fellow! Pooh! Wanting to get you thrown out he was – he who's tempted four good Methodists from Salutation Street to that trumpery little heathen place on the cliff where they don't even sing the proper hymns. Sacrilege – that's what it is. I'm sure my poor husband would turn in his grave if he knew. Yes, indeed. Joseph was such a worker for Salutation Street. T'would break his heart, it would."

"All that – in the name of religion!" Stephen said to Julia

later. "Still, on the whole it's a good thing for us they have their little wars – at least we can be sure of *some* backing."

For some time after this Joe Traill's argument with Mrs Tremayne diverted local interest and antipathy from the school, since the two chapels were involved, claiming the publicity for themselves. In the meantime Andrea continued, with the help of the Countess, to keep Marianne as much as possible under her wing, letting the girl sleep at her own studio so that she had to spend no time alone going to and from the classes.

Naturally, under these circumstances, Stephen began to see more of Andrea, drawn to her through sympathy of mutual purpose, and the realisation that this girl, after all, was neither so selfish nor cold as she appeared.

"Remember," he said to her one day, "if you get nervy about things at all, I mean if there should ever be any incident when you're out with Marianne, you must tell me, and we'll have to make some other arrangement for her."

Andrea shrugged. "Nervy?" she said. "I've got nerves of steel. Don't worry, they don't bother *me*. In a way I rather enjoy it all."

"Why?" asked Stephen, interested.

"Perhaps because I can appreciate it," Andrea admitted, "the cruelty, I mean. It's kind of savage and strange, but it suits this place. I know what they feel – the natives. They resent us. Why shouldn't they? *I* should if I'd belonged here for centuries. Why, it's in the very air and rocks, haven't you felt it? You would, if you'd been on those wild cliffs near Praille at night. Have you?"

"No, not yet, I've not had time," he admitted.

"You should make time," she said. "I think you'd like it."

"Why do you think that?"

"Because *you're* merciless too," she replied.

"Merciless? How? In what way?"

She was silent for a moment, then went on, "You'll get what you want. But you can't afford to have a heart."

He stared at her. "A bit brutal, aren't you?"

She laughed shortly. "Meant as a compliment. *I* haven't a heart either."

For a second, watching her, he believed her. There was

something pagan about the clear cool quality of her stare, the pale flawless skin and green eyes, that held him fascinated by its contempt for human feeling. His senses were stirred. He visualised painting her as some creature of the sea itself washed up into a hidden cove. Already he had the finished canvas in mind: visualised her white in the moonlight, her pale hair spread like weed over the rocks.

He jerked himself back to earth abruptly.

"Hearts or no," he said lightly, "I must get back to Julia. I'm late, and if I remember correctly she's got something extra nice to eat."

He said goodbye to her, but his mind was exhilarated, confused. Until that brief conversation he'd liked her. Now he was stirred by completely different emotions, and because of it there was a faint guilty feeling at his heart when Julia greeted him at the door ten minutes later. The sensation was undeserved and unwarranted. He knew he loved Julia and would always love her, but after all there were other things than loving a person. All manner of contacts were necessary for enlarging one's viewpoints and knowledge of life.

Thus Stephen justified himself.

Chapter Eight

October flamed along the cliffs and moors above Praille when Stephen suggested to Julia one day that it might be a good idea to give a dramatic evening at the studio.

"Plays, do you mean?" she asked.

"Yes," he said thoughtfully. "And I thought perhaps you could write one for us – you belonged to the Linchester Players Society, didn't you? And did a bit of producing. So you know the ropes. What about it? There are local legends that could be adapted – something Cornish but not too serious. Savvy?"

"Perhaps," she agreed, with her mind reeling.

"You see," he went on, "we might break down the local barriers that way, get the people interested."

"If we could do it, yes," she replied. "But how do we know they'd come? Probably they wouldn't."

"If they were in it themselves, they might."

"Oh, I *see*. You mean, let *them* act."

"Yes – Trevaskiss and his lot. Oh, he mightn't himself – he's too touchy and getting on. But he's got a daughter and two sons, and you know, there isn't much for young folk to do here in an evening. What do you think, Julia?"

"It might work," she admitted. "It would be quite fun. When I first saw the studio I thought it rather theatrical and romantic-looking. Yes, I *do* agree, Stephen."

"Good. Get on with an idea then, and I'll broach the matter to Trevaskiss."

And so, before another month had passed, plans were already underway for a Winter Show. Julia was secretly amazed and faintly envious of the way in which her husband had managed the little group of Cornish people, who had been prevailed upon by his charm and against their own puritanical instincts to take part in the play. The fact that such an occasion would be one up on the rival chapel's Social Club, was also, no doubt, a guiding factor, and the more so since it had been arranged for the proceeds to go towards the Distressed Fishermen's Welfare Fund.

"The trouble is," Julia said one day, "it'll cost a bit, Stephen. It always does. There are always certain props and things that have to be bought, and you know our money's dribbling down a bit quicker than we thought. There was the extra blanket I had to get, and paying for mending the roof."

He frowned. "All the same, we ought to be *well* in now. I'm earning money, and the Countess stands the rent for the studio."

"I know. But you spend more, darling. The books and things, and – well – the drinks you buy for other people. I know you feel you have to do it, but it all mounts up."

"Anyhow," said Stephen, "we've got to launch out a bit, so there's no point in being skinflint at this juncture. Besides, I'm sure the Countess would back us over any additional expense. She's interested in the show."

"But we shouldn't depend on *her* always," Julia said sharply. "Oh, Stephen, shouldn't we go slowly until we can stand on our own feet?"

"Throw it up, you mean?" he queried. "The dramatics?"

"No. I didn't mean that quite."

"Well, you can't have it both ways," he said, irritated.

In the end Julia gave in to him, and a fortnight later, by the light of an oil lamp, the first reading of her play – a whimsical fantasy with a good deal of comedy about it – was held in Stephen's studio.

The Countess was present, and was frankly and genuinely surprised at Julia's achievement.

"But, my dear child, it's really good," she said. "You have talent. And I like the naughty bits. I didn't expect it of you."

"Of course she didn't," Julia said to Stephen later, "she just thought me a fool. I told you that before."

On the whole the evening was a success, and warmed by the

beer supplied by Stephen, even Travaskiss himself was prevailed upon to take the part of an old piskie-led farmer.

"After this," Stephen said to Julia on their way home,
"you'll be able to take things in hand yourself and arrange
several dos a year."

"What do you mean?" she asked. "Do it on my own?"

"Why not? Wouldn't you like to?"

"Well, in a way, but – oh, Stephen, it was to be a *mutual*
affair."

"But, darling, I've so many other things on, and – "

"What other things?" she asked quickly.

"Running a group isn't all play, you know," he told her.
"There's the Winter Exhibition to get arranged, and I haven't
done a thing for it myself. Be fair."

"I'm trying to be," she agreed dubiously.

"If you won't co-operate, say so," Stephen said sharply,
"and we'll drop the whole idea."

"Oh, no. I'll do it," said Julia. "It's only that – well, I
haven't had a lot of experience at producing. It's a responsibility, having to think of everything myself."

"Now that's just silly," he stated. "I shall look in quite a lot,
and if you brought out all those plays at your school as you
said, and then the Linchester Players – "

"That was quite different. They were ordinary people, and
these aren't. The old man . . ."

"Folk like him will make it all the easier," he prophesied.
"Supply their own humour."

Afterwards, when she came to think it over, Julia agreed
with Stephen that the project might be rather fun. It was true
she'd not had any active outside interests of her own since her
marriage, and this new venture might stimulate her to further
efforts at writing. A point in its favour.

And so play readings and rehearsals were soon underway,
and Julia found herself enjoying them, although conscious at
times that number seven was being consequently neglected,
that their meals were becoming more and more haphazard,
and that Stephen was forced to eat our more freequently, an
item which drew further upon their funds. Meanwhile
Stephen's picture – a secret affair, done for the most part at the
Countess's studio because the light was bett , and privacy

43

more assured – was apparently progressing well.

He would tell Julia nothing about it, and assured her that no one else had seen it.

"But you just wait," he said, "you wait, darling, you'll be surprised."

Julia did not concern herself unduly about it, telling herself it was after all natural Stephen should want to surprise her. But towards the beginning of November something happened.

One evening when Julia had gone to rehearsal, and Stephen to work on his painting, old Traevaskiss and his son did not turn up at the studio, but sent a message to say they both had colds and wouldn't be there that week. This meant that the rehearsal would have to be postponed since they were taking major parts. Accordingly, when they'd drunk the hot drinks which Julia always supplied, the other three players said good night and left. It was by then only a quarter past eight, and her husband wouldn't be back for another hour and a half. She tidied up, looked through a few of Stephen's drawings, and presently locked up the studio and left.

She intended going straight back, but the night was clear and fine with no wind and only the suspicion of frost in the air. On second thoughts she decided to take a short walk first, and instead of cutting down to Crab Street to turn along by the harbour. Out at sea the lights of the fishing fleet twinkled like stars on the water. The very stillness was exciting, broken only by the occasional tramp of fishermen's feet and the lazy quiet lapping of the waves on the beach. At the far end of the harbour, by the quay, the lamps of a cafe shone invitingly and she decided to look in and have a coffee.

She walked briskly along while the sharp air brought a fresh colour to her cheeks. Her eyes sparkled under her small fur cap, and she wished she'd brought her muff. It was getting colder.

She went straight into the cafe and sat down. At first she thought there was no one else there. Then something impelled her to look round, and for a brief second she could not believe her eyes. Surely she had made some mistake? But no. There, half hidden in the shadows behind a beaded curtain, sat – Stephen! And yes, there could be no mistake, Andrea.

44

When he saw her Stephen jumped up and came into the open, surprise and something else – something faintly guilty – upon his face, but his voice was warm and welcoming as though it was the most delightful thing in the world finding her there.

"Julia, love, how nice. Come and join us, or shall we join you?"

Really his equilibrium was amazing! In a steady voice, but with a queer sick feeling in her heart, Julia answered, "It doesn't matter which, I suppose. But I thought you were painting?"

"And I thought you were rehearsing," he said.

She laughed shortly. "So we were both mistaken."

She thought she saw a faint gleam of discomfiture in his eyes, and was about to continue in a sharper vein when Andrea came up languidly.

"Hullo," she said, with faint mockery. "I hope you don't mind my stealing your husband for half an hour? Really, it's not so bad as it looks."

Before her cool insolence Julia wilted momentarily. She felt humiliated, tongue-tied. Her composure deserted her, leaving her feeling very much like a small child about to break into a storm of sobbing. She felt her lip tremble then pulled herself together. As if she minded Stephen sitting with a woman in a cafe! Only he might have told her about it first, so that her dignity could have been prepared, forearmed.

"I don't know what you mean," she said shortly, and Andrea had the grace to flush slightly.

The rest of the little interim was hardly enjoyable. Yet there was no reason, Stephen told himself with irritation, to feel guilty, no plausible excuse for Julia's stony look. He knew that look – it meant trouble, and generally, heralded a scene. Well, for once she wouldn't get it. If she raged, he'd let her. After all, what was wrong in having a friendly tête-à-tête with one's model? The problem was that Julia didn't know Andrea *was* his model and probably suspected worse.

"Well," he said, on their way home, "you needn't have looked such daggers. I'm sure Andrea noticed."

"Did she? What of it?" Julia said, with an upward thrust of

45

her chin. "It doesn't matter in the slightest to me *what* she thinks."

"It ought to then," Stephen said doggedly. "You're not a child."

"I don't think," Julia said in a clear hard little voice, "you consider *my* feelings in the slightest nowadays."

"Don't be foolish."

"Well, do you?"

"I don't know what you mean."

"I think you might have told me," she went on, "that your painting hours were really rendezvous with Andrea. I don't say I should have liked it, but I should at least have respected your honesty."

His voice changed. "You've got it all wrong. Our little rendezvous, as you call it, was the end of something."

"Of what? A love affair?"

"My God, what a mind you've got!"

"Tell me," she insisted coldly.

"I've been painting her. She's been my model for the picture – the picture for the exhibition. And tonight it was finished. Another thing you'd better get into your pretty head once and for all – if I want to have a chat with Andrea or any other girl over a drink of coffee or something stronger, I'm free to do it. You're my wife, but not my keeper. Understand?"

"You've made it quite clear."

"Up to date, however," he resumed with chill sarcasm, "I've remained safely tied to your apron strings. All the same, have a care, my love, and don't let that wicked little temper of yours spoil things."

It was a warning, and in her overwrought state it seemed to her his love was already fading. She'd given more importance to the incident with Andrea than was warranted, but Stephen's tone to her now – the harsh edge to his voice, and curl of his lip – was proof somehow that already, during the short period of their marriage, they were drifting apart.

"Oh, Stephen," she said, struggling with her tears.

"Spare the dramatics," he remarked, unrelenting, not even taking her arm.

Later, when they got back, the rift remained. They lay in

46

bed with no kiss or gesture of tenderness between them.

The next day more normal relationships were established; Stephen attempted a half-apology, and she admitted she had been rather childish. But the issue was left unresolved. A lingering doubt remained in Julia's mind. All that morning, when Stephen was away, she tried to erase it, but reassurance evaded her. The lovely thing – her belief in Stephen – was threatened for the first time. Though she didn't fully recognise it, the affair, trivial in itself, marked a turning point in her life. The last frail pristine qualify of childhood fell away, and she emerged as a woman who must take on her own responsibilities, facing what disillusions life might hold yet still somehow carving a future to her own needs.

As she stood by the window thinking, her face hardened; in profile a proud determined face. So might she look when she was much older, and had lived to the full, savouring all that fate could do.

Gradually some of the tension fell away, and a new strength came to her. Whatever happened – even though the future might not be easy, though unhappiness too was there – she would work out a satisfactory pattern for mutual existence.

Chapter Nine

For the next few weeks Julia flung herself with forced interest into the plays, wilfully shutting her eyes to the lack of understanding which had existed between herself and Stephen since the Andrea episode. True, they were superficially amicable when occasion warranted it. He still desired her, though she thought frequently that he made love to her more as a right – the male perogative – than with romantic longing. Was he really so blind, she wondered frequently, that he did not sense something was missing? It seemed so. To save her own pride and dignity she made an outward attempt to match her mood to his, although in solitary moments she occasionally shed a few tears. The shadow of Andrea remained. Since that November night the subject hadn't arisen, and she doubted now it ever would. Just how much of the girl Stephen saw those days, Julia didn't know, and she told herself she did not care. But when Stephen was very late back, or during the hours he spent away from her, she was intuitively jealous.

She recognised that the painting – the one Stephen had envisioned, of Andrea on the shore – was the most striking he'd done, and at the beginning of December it was hung together with work by other Cornish artists in the rather ramshackle gallery used at that time. This was prior to the show at his own studio, and brought him a certain amount of kudos and publicity.

Shortly before Christmas the play was given, and was a success. It did what had been intended – united the Stephen Kerr School with a certain element of the fishing fraternity.

The Countess was delighted, commending him with vulgar good humour.

"You've done it, my dear," she said. "Stephen love, I'm proud of you. If I were a younger woman, I'd sleep with you for this."

Julia winced as their sponsor turned to her, playfully tapping the young wife's hand. "No offence, dear – didn't meant it. A silly creature I am, and I'm sure this young man of ours wouldn't have got half so far without you."

Ours, Julia thought. How dare she? And how *can* Stephen suck up to her like he does? She was learning day by day that he was capable of doing many things she wouldn't have suspected.

Christmas came, and was spent in a round of parties – at the Countess's and Andrea's, and with one thrown at the studio. Stephen appeared to enjoy himself. But Julia was not happy. Christmas to her symbolised a time of good will, simple fun and faith, when one could become a child again and enjoy log fires, crackers, and the hundred and one other things that gave the season atmosphere; a time to be remembered years ahead in maturity and old age. But Christmas at Port Todric consisted mainly of listening to the Countess's bawdy stories, or watching the shadows play upon Andrea's lovely cheekbones, with the consciousness that Stephen was watching them too. Yes, Andrea was beautiful, Julia had to admit it, and the beauty hurt like a light that couldn't be caught – holding the poignant faraway echo of some wild strange song, stirring the senses to desire. No wonder Stephen was ensnared. Or was he? Over and over again the tantalising question returned.

I shall never know, Julia thought, we may come close again, and be happy, but I shall never know exactly what he feels for her – what there is between them.

There were times when unreasoning jealousy was so strong she felt she couldn't bear it. However, she did. And somehow December passed into January. Then February came – a wild wet month with gales which tore at the cliffs and harbour, followed by weeks of bitter cold when it was impossible to keep the badly heated rooms warm, and Julia's hands ached from chilblains and peeling vegetables in the icy water.

49

One of the students left Stephen's school at Christmas, but since then the Countess herself had become an active member which meant that he spent even more time away from his wife.

Following classes there was generally some matter to be discussed with his sponsor, and frequently a pressing invitation to a drink at her studio. Julia was thrown more and more upon herself, and as her loneliness grew became embittered with the irritations of housework. Her temper sharpened, and the few moments she spent with Stephen were frequently spoiled by senseless arguments and quarrelling. Realising that if they went on in that way much longer the inevitable break up would take place, she flung herself mechanically into the effort of writing a new novel as diversion and outlet. But the work was forced and unreal. She knew, even when she sent it away to the publisher at the beginning of April, that it fell far short of *Bitter Wind*, and when it was returned to her a fortnight later she was not surprised.

Enclosed with the rejection slip, however, was a personal letter from the publisher himself.

Stephen had already gone to the studio when the post came, but Julia had not yet cleared away the breakfast things. For some moments she sat at the table with the note in front of her. It was significant and to the point. But it was more than that – it was a challenge to her honesty, to those very things which were the basis of her marriage with Stephen.

I am sorry to tell you I can make no offer for your latest book which does not do justice to your literary capacity. Generally it is the other way round – a writer gains, through knowledge of life. But your observations seem trivial and the characterisation unreal. Perhaps you have not had sufficient time to write what you really feel, perhaps you are tired. Whatever the reason, dear Miss Benson, try and bring self-criticism to your work – see it objectively from the outside. Perhaps I should not say all this, but believe me, it is only because I think so highly of your potential, and because of the startling merit of *Bitter Wind* that I do so. I shall be pleased at any time to read more of your work, when you have got your pen into perspective again. And this I am sure you will do. A good writer is not easily discouraged.

Believe me, I remain,

Yours sincerely,
Michael Darrett

At first she felt rebuffed, hurt, and tired. Impulsively she was about to screw up the note and destroy it when she read it through again. And then slowly she realised he was right. The story *was* trivial and cheap, she *was* out of perspective. This second book was a tawdry, worthless affair that had never been worth starting. Was it then that her marriage itself was becoming tawdry and useless? And if so, why? And what was to be done about it?

All that morning, at odd moments, the past swept over her poignantly: the day of their marriage, the sweetness of those first weeks together – the fun they'd had, and the promises and belief in each other! The difficulties had not mattered then, because they'd cared so much. Neither had it been important that she was not writing; living came first. But if going on as they were meant being second rate at both things – marriage *and* work – then surely it was better to sacrifice the first that the second could at least have a chance?

These revelations gave her a strange feeling of detachment and unreality.

This can't be me, she thought once, looking at herself in the glass, this cold callous creature weighing the pros and cons of my married life.

But of course it wasn't only that – it went much deeper. It had come down to a matter of stark fundamental values, an issue which, even had she wanted to, she could no longer turn aside. For the first time she was facing herself squarely, and the question in her mind was not a pretty one.

Is love worth it? she queried of herself. Is Stephen himself worth the sacrifice of your own brain? Is his work really so important after all? For a whole year you've sacrificed yourself for his school, made yourself tired looking after him, forcing yourself into spheres you hate, denying your own capacities. And all for this – misunderstanding and jealousy, fear and bitterness, with moments of passion thrown in. What about yourself? You are cleverer than Stephen, and you know it, yet you're simply being *used*.

That same afternoon he returned from the school to fetch a book he'd left behind. He looked rather tired; she noticed that his face was thinner than it used to be, that a certain amount of boyishness had gone from it. And yet – when he turned to say goodbye to her there was something of the old look in his eyes, and she thought, with the spring of hope reviving: It can't be too late. Behind it all he loves me still, I'm sure he does.

Impulsively she said, "Stephen?"

"Yes, Julia?"

"I want to talk to you tonight. There's something I need to say. Will you come back as soon as possible?"

He looked surprised. "Of course. But if it's important, tell me now."

She shook her head. "No, Stephen, tonight."

When he had gone she felt happier than she'd done for a long time, realising that she should have tackled the matter before in this way, and had it out with him.

She expected Stephen back at six, and directly after tea went out for a walk, feeling the need of exercise and sunshine. From the harbour she cut up to the left along the cliffs towards Praille, behind which there rose the moors peaked by the wild hills where the Druids once worshipped, outlined now by the jagged silhouettes of ancient tin mine remains.

Always along there she felt herself responding in a queer atavistic way to the surroundings. The gaunt country – something primitive and pagan which went deeper than small personal issues – struck a chord of sympathy in her which released her spirit and made her free for a time from worrying problems and unhappiness. The agelessness of the coast claimed her, and walking there, in the solitude, it seemed to her how minute were the little desires and perplexities of men who were for a time on the earth, then disappeared from it after what was, comparatively, but a few short seconds in the face of eternity.

Curiously, there was an odd kind of comfort in these reflections which clarified her emotions into some sort of perspective. That afternoon, when she had walked for half an hour or so, she turned and made her way back, feeling that whatever accrued from her talk with Stephen, she would at least be able to face it with composure. Nevertheless, when she approached the house shortly before six there was again that odd jumping of her heart, a certain excited anticipation which she could not entirely control.

She hurried up the steps, running up the last one or two. Obviously he had returned; the curtain had been pulled slightly over one side of the window to shield the room from the bright sunshine.

Inside she paused, stood quite still, the smile dying on her lips, the gladness gone from her eyes in one quick second.

Stephen was there, but he was not alone. Half lying across the sofa was Andrea.

Stephen had already laid the table and placed there the salad Julia had prepared earlier. Now he was busy making coffee at the stove.

"Hullo, Julia," he said with apparent welcome. "I thought I'd surprise you – make the coffee now. You don't mind, do you? I'm deuced thirsty, and so's Andrea. I brought her along with me because we had the next show to discuss, and thought you might be able to advise us over the hanging. You see . . ."

He stopped, aware that Julia had not moved, that her face was very white and her mouth strangely set, that she was looking at him almost belligerently.

"Is anything wrong? What's the matter?" he asked innocently.

She fought for control, to remain silent until the polite perfunctory trivialities could be assumed. But her quick temper let her down.

Stephen had done this to her – on top of everything else he had forgotten apparently that she had requested him to come back early for a special reason. And he had *promised*. She had returned full of hope and constructive planning, thinking they were to be alone for once. And what did she find? Another woman, the woman who had subtly become her enemy, ensconced there in *her* home, about to eat from *her* table.

Anger deepened. Her jaw tightened. "Had you forgotten,"

she said coldly, "that we had something important to discuss, Stephen?"

"Oh! Had we? Yes, I'm sorry, you did say something, I remember now. But still, never mind. It can wait until later."

"I'm afraid it can't wait," Julia said, throwing discretion to the wind.

Andrea jumped up. "You mean I'm de trop?" she queried in quiet, amused tones.

Stephen reddened. "Of course you're not. Sit down. Julia's being childish."

"I think you'd better go," Julia stated recklessly, "if you don't mind."

"Oh, certainly. I'd hate to disturb the domestic nest."

"Stay here," Stephen insisted. "You'll do nothing of the sort."

Andrea gave a short laugh. "My dear Stephen, if you imagine I'm going to stay put and become the target of a domestic scene, you're grossly mistaken. I don't appreciate the role at all. Goodbye. Keep your end up."

She picked up her coat, and a few seconds later, with one last amused, half-contemptuous glance, had opened the door and slipped out. The patter of her sandals could be heard running down the steps. Then there was a silence, a taut angry silence, before Stephen wheeled round on Julia.

"And just what do you think you're doing?"

"What I should have done a long time ago," she flashed, "turning that woman out of my house."

"Incidentally, it's my house too, and I won't have you behaving to my friends in such a disgusting manner. You humiliated and shamed me. Understand?" His voice rose, as he repeated, "I won't *have* it."

Julia stood rigid and unmoving. "And what do you propose to do about it?" she asked.

He took her by the shoulders, shaking her, causing a long strand of her red-brown hair to fall free from the net about her shoulders.

She wrenched herself away. "Let me go! How dare you touch me? *Stephen*! Let me go."

"You need a damn' good spanking," he said, "that's what's the matter with you. You're just plain spoiled."

"Oh, don't be ridiculous! Just because I make an effort at getting our lives straight – "

"Straight?" he sneered. "You call *this* getting our lives straight? Insulting my friends, and showing such jealousy that – honest-to-God, Julia! I think you must be off your head."

The anger died from her voice suddenly. "No," she said almost lifelessly, "I'm quite sane, Stephen. I may be fighting for something, I may be fighting in the wrong way, but I'm sane. I see things quite clearly – too clearly, perhaps. The harridan I'm becoming, your growing dislike of home life . . ."

"Well, no wonder, considering the endless rows there've been lately."

She was silent for a minute, then went on, "Have you ever thought there might be a *reason* for it all, Stephen? Have you ever once put yourself in my shoes, wondered what it's like for me here, alone so much, and knowing that you were content for it to be that way – content to go on giving your time and attention to people whom you know really aren't worth it?"

"I don't know what you mean."

"Yes, you do. If you had the slightest respect for them – the Countess and her cronies who are, as you say, putting you on your own feet – it wouldn't be so bad."

"Don't try and gull yourself," he said quickly. "Don't try and mask your behaviour under a pretext of fine feeling, because it won't wash, Julia. You know very well that your main trouble is jealousy. As I said before, you're just crazily jealous, and that's all there is to it."

She shrugged. "If that's how you feel – well – I suppose that ends it."

"Ends what?"

"There's not much point in going on with our marriage, is there, if you feel that way? I mean, if you're so obviously in love with Andrea and so out of love with me – " She broke off, with a sob in her throat.

He groaned impatiently. "Who said I was in love with Andrea? Nonsense! Utter rubbish!"

"Then why must you see so much of her? Oh, Stephen, you're obviously attracted."

"That's different." He was sullen.

"Well, we don't seem to be doing much good, do we, by talking? I'd planned to get things straight between us, but – "

"You seem to have done pretty well," he told her with cold sarcasm.

She didn't reply, but after a pause continued, "Stephen, I've been thinking. At the moment I just can't go on like this any more."

"What then? What's the answer?"

"I must go away," she said.

"*Away*?"

"For a time," she said, "a month, perhaps a bit longer – just to think things out."

"Ridiculous," he said quickly, "quite ridiculous."

"Why?"

"Expense for one thing. Then the look of the thing. Also – you're my wife. Why should you leave me?"

"Because I happen to be an individual too," she said sharply. "You may have married me, Stephen, but my soul's my own still. At least, I hope so."

"How very dramatic."

"Maybe. But I mean it. I'm sick of this life, as it is now. I've got to have time on my own."

"You're being childish."

"*No*. I've grown up."

For a few minutes he stared at her, speechless. Her composure defeated him, the defiance of her rigid figure maddened him, stirring him to irrational anger. He could not understand her newly-found detached composure. When she was temperamental, angry, he could deal with her. But this aloof, calm decisiveness – the hard, almost calculating look in her eyes – was beyond him. It was also a challenge to his manhood. Though tenderness at that moment was far from him – perhaps because of it – possession, the old primitive instinct, came to life in him suddenly. He would show her how things were, who was master. Said she was leaving him, did she? The idea!

He took her by the arm, felt her flinch under the cream gabardine of her coat.

Then, forcing her to look at him, he said in a voice she had never heard from him before, a thick trembling voice, "You'll do just what I say, understand? You're my wife, and you'd better remember it."

"Let me go."

But his force increased. "Why should I?"

After a moment or two, however, he freed her and pushed her into a chair. She sat there, half fascinated, half frightened, watching him as he went over to the cabinet and took from it a bottle of whisky and two glasses.

He had two drinks himself, before bringing one to her. "Have it – do you good."

"No thanks."

She pushed his hand away, and the glass fell to the floor, where the spirit trickled in a stream through the carpet.

Stephen laughed, and his hand closed on her shoulder again. "You know, Julia," he said, "you are a little fool. It's a pity." He forced her to her feet. "So you'll toddle off on your little own, will you?"

She struggled against him. "Stop it, Stephen."

The renewed contact was all that was needed to inflame him to action. He lifted her up and carried her to the bed, fumbling with hot hands at the bodice and waistband of her dress.

For some minutes she fought him, not knowing what drove her – anger, despair or hatred, intermixed with a bitter love. But at last, when he'd taken her ruthlessly, she lay quietened and exhausted, and presently Stephen, too, was still upon the bed.

After some time had elapsed he turned and said, "Julia?"

But she did not reply; she lay with eyes fixed in front of her, something in them he had never seen before. Soon he got up and dressed. Julia heard him moving about the room, then a little later picking up his coat and going out. She did not move. She still lay there as though carved from stone, but her mind was active. It was all quite clear. She knew what she must do.

The next morning at breakfast time Stephen looked mildly ashamed of himself, while Julia sat with her features frozen and hard.

"Don't be a martyr," he said. "Be human. I'm sorry."

But all she said was, "It's quite all right," in a tone which implied only too clearly that everything wasn't.

Stephen sighed. "Oh, very well – if you *must* play the injured innocent."

She did not deign to reply.

Shortly afterwards Stephen went to the studio, and Julia was left to go ahead with the plan she had thought out during the long night hours when she had lain wakeful and distraught, considering the wretched state of her marriage and Stephen's brutality in particular. It was not that she had resented his possession of her. The outrage, in her mind, lay in the manner of it: that he should have respected her so little in the face of what had gone before – Andrea's intrusion and his defence of it. However tactless she herself had been, however badly she had mismanaged the affair – and she knew only too well the shortcomings of her own quick temper – the fact remained that they could go on no longer as they were. Certainly *she* could not. Her own pride forbade it. If Stephen thought so little of her that he could behave as he had, then they *must* separate until any possible future was clear.

A queer numbed sense of fatalism possessed her as she packed a few things into a portmanteau, tidied up the room and wrote the short note which half an hour later she left on the table.

Dear Stephen,

I meant what I said last night. I am very unhappy. And until I can get things into perspective again, I'm leaving. When everything's clear to me I'll write to you. But until then don't try to find me. It's no good. If I see Mrs Tremayne I shall tell her I've had a telegram to go and see a sick aunt.

Goodbye Stephen, I've put your clean shirt to air on the small table in the sun by the window.

Julia

When she lugged her portmanteau down the steps there was no sign of Mrs T, for which she was grateful. Now that the moment had come she felt the tears of emotion and reaction very near. However, battling with her bag, the business of finding a boy to carry it to the small station, of seeing that she had enough money in her purse to pay for the expenses which must lie ahead, and the whole fuss of looking up trains, deciding where to go and getting her ticket, forced her into a comparatively practical state of mind, and forty minutes later when the train moved out of the station, she was amazed at her control.

She had never been to Trelissey, but she'd heard of it and at the booking hall had discovered that there was a through train almost immediately which arrived there after half an hour.

From what she'd seen of the place in guide books, she knew that it was quaint and tiny, a favourite haunt of artists and writers, and that there were one or two small guesthouses and an inn there. It was unlikely she would fail to find accommodation at one or the other.

Sitting in the dusty compartment, with her bag on the seat beside her, she was surprised as the train chugged away to find herself so suddenly composed and capable of making the break. Any impulse to weep or give way to emotional regret had completely faded. She was tired, of course, more tired than she had known, and the freedom from complexity, from the endless questioning, had left a vacuum in her mind which in itself was a kind of peace. And yet a few months ago how incredible it would have seemed to her that a time would come when she would be able to act like this on her own initiative, apart from Stephen.

She watched the sea disappear then come into view again at odd points as they passed small grey villages and tracts of moorland, while a sense of unreality grew upon her. At the third station the inspector came round and told her, "Trelissey – next stop," while he punched her ticket and smiled at her. The smile was friendly, genuine. It warmed her, and she began to feel alive again.

Quite soon they were off once more, and presently the train drew up and she got out. Seeing her standing there with her bag on the platform, a young porter came to her assistance.

"Where for, miss?" he enquired. "Like your bag carrying?"

Julia explained that she had not booked anywhere, but that she wanted accommodation in Trelissey.

"The Blue Dolphin, miss," he said. "That's the place to try. You'll get in there sure 'nough. A real nice place, the Blue Dolphin. John Gauntry'd fix you up there."

"Very well," Julia said, "thank you. Is it far – I mean, shall I need a carriage or cab or something?"

The porter scratched his ear. "Well, now – just at the moment there beant be anything like that around," he said, considering. "But if you felt you could walk like – it's not far, miss – and I'd be carrying the luggage for you."

"That's all right then," Julia agreed.

"Good. And I can take you to Mr Gauntry myself. A fine fellow, Mr Gauntry."

As she followed him out of the station Julia hoped that the Blue Dolphin would not be beyond her means. And as she considered finance she remembered suddenly that she had not told Stephen she'd taken the petty cash from the box.

Still, she told herself, he'd be sure to guess, and if he didn't he would soon find out. She could hardly have gone without money; all the same it wasn't very much. Ten pounds only. Enough to see her through a week or two, but after that . . . Oh, well, she thought, I'm not going to worry about tomorrow. I suppose there are things I could do, if it came to it.

"This way," the porter said, turning a corner abruptly outside the station, "down the hill we go."

Julia saw before her a steep cobbled street clustered with cottages and whitewashed houses, leading down to the glimmer of sea and a small harbour at the bottom. A wave of apple blossom scent and lilac came to meet her, and an old man with a donkey cart selling vegetables touched his cap to her as she passed.

But this is lovely – *lovely*, she thought, with delight. If only circumstances were different, if only the muddled months could be washed away as though they had never been!

Halfway down the street they came to the doorway of a very ancient inn, which led into the hall from under a pillared stone porch. A kindly-looking elderly man with short side whiskers was smoking a pipe outside.

"Marnin', Mr Gauntry," the porter said. "Got any rooms, sir? This young lady be wanting to stay in Trelissey for a bit."

Gauntry gave one quick look at Julia, smiled and said,

"Well now, I think so, yes. You wanting to stay long, my dear?"

"A few weeks, perhaps," Julia said cautiously.

"Come in," he said. "I'll speak of Mrs Hocking."

Five minutes later Julia found herself in a low-ceilinged beamed bedroom smelling of lavender and old wood, with the suspicion from below of malt. The window was open, and through it, to the right, she glimpsed the narrow harbour clearly, with its glittering quiet water on which the small fishing boats rested like toys. Smaller, gentler than Port Todric, Trelissey with its flowers and blossom seemed to her like a dream. She recollected the helpfulness of the porter, and the welcoming smile of John Gauntry and his housekeeper. Yes, this was a place of friendship – a kind place.

Her eyes clouded with tears for a moment. It seemed too long since she had known real kindness.

Chapter Ten

For the next few days Julia did not allow herself to think deeply, was content merely with the freedom from strain, the dreamy sense of negation which now possessed her. The inn was smaller inside than she had imagined, and at the moment only two other guests were staying there – a grey-haired maiden lady who went out sketching in the mornings, and a tired-looking middle-aged man, whom she gathered quite soon was a writer. The fact was verified later by John Gauntry who told her his name was Travers, Humphrey Travers.

"Do you mean – do you mean *the* Humphrey Travers?" Julia asked.

Gauntry nodded. "Stays here some months every year, Mrs Kerr," he told her. "His books are thought a lot of up country, I believe."

"Oh, *yes*," she gasped. "He's – why, he's very famous."

"Ah, well, no one would know it from his manner," the landlord told her. "A quieter man you couldn't find, my dear. But then, that's often so. The more a man can do, the less he talks about it."

"I suppose so," Julia said thoughtfully.

That same evening, over the intimacies of coffee in the lounge, Humphrey Travers spoke to her. Their conversation consisted only of the most temporal slight things – the magnolia trees in the garden opposite, the coming into harbour that afternoon of two French crabbers, the appreciation of Mrs Hocking's excellent coffee. But it was a beginning. It was a relief to Julia to be spoken to by a man who might have stepped out of her own late grandfather's drawing room.

After the months of bitter drudgery it was a pleasant change, which reacted to her rather in the manner of a soothing drug, indicating that her femininity, if not yet her brain, was being – however unconsciously – appreciated. The knowledge fortified and cheered her. Looking at herself in the glass before going down to dinner, she'd been surprised to find that unhappiness had not put a greater mark on her, that no lines of strain marred her looks or spoiled the youthful freshness of her face.

She was wearing a simple, tightly-waisted, grey frock that had been her afternoon gown for tea parties in Linchester. Since her marriage she'd only worn it occasionally. Now she wondered why. Its pale colouring brought out the reddish tints in her hair, and emphasised the glow of her clear skin. The fact that excitement and inner fatigue had brightened her eyes, only added to the general impression of youthful vitalilty and grace.

The next day they met accidentally on a walk, and strolled back together for lunch.

Later, choosing her words carefully, she subtly opened the subject of writing, and found, delightedly, that he had read, and thought quite highly of, *Bitter Wind*.

"Of course," he said honestly, "if flags in parts, the standard of language – from a literary point of view, I mean – is at a higher level sometimes than at others. But for a first book it's good, and you certainly ought to keep your hand in now – follow it up with another. That is, if you've any ideas to go upon?"

"Oh, yes, I have," Julia spoke quickly. There was a pause, then she went on a little more tentatively, "I did as a matter of fact write one this year. But it wasn't any good."

"Oh?"

"But I think it was because my heart wasn't in it," she confided on impulse. "At the time, you see, I was very unhappy."

He shook his head. "To be conscious of unhappiness is no good to a writer," he told her, "not as a background for creating anything worthwhile. *After* the unhappiness, yes, that's a different matter. But when a real work is created – something big that will live – the author should be oblivious of himself. He may, in the first place, have been stirred by an injustice, or some dream, some emotional experience which has touched him deeply. But when once he's got it going, his limited personal reaction is at the most a very secondary part."

"Yes, I think I see what you mean," Julia said slowly.

This was only the first of many such conversations. As the days slipped by Julia found herself turning more and more to Humphrey Travers' gentle companionship. Soon she had unburdened a little of the story of her unhappy marriage, and found afterwards that the friendship was easier. He seemed to understand the long silences which sometimes came upon her, when she could not talk because of the bitter ache of remembering Stephen.

Once he said to her, "I think you took the right course. No use having second rate things in your life. Although of course – " and he smiled disarmingly "– we sometimes think they are, when they are not."

"What do you mean?" asked Julia, clutching at the straw of hope.

"Life is largely a matter of understanding, you know," Travers told her. "It's possible to be too near to a thing to be able to judge correctly, like looking at one's face too closely in a contorting mirror. That's why I said I thought you'd done what was right in getting away to view things more objectively. You may find, after a lapse of time, that you see things differently. It would be a pity to throw something good away just through misunderstanding."

"Yes, but I'm afraid it's all gone too far," Julia replied sadly.

At the end of the second week Travers was called away to London and Julia was flung once more upon her own resources.

She realised with dismay that her money was quickly going and that she had come to no conclusion concerning her future course of action. The thought of having to write to Stephen for assistance was repugnant to her. Her independence and stubborn will were in revolt at the mere suggestion. If she'd met him one day by chance – or if he'd found her and offered – well, that was a different matter. But the odds were all against that. In all probability he was no longer terribly concerned about her, was content for her to go her own way so long as she didn't trouble him. The idea depressed her. It was a dreadful thought – the most dreadful because the days were so achingly beautiful just then, warm and windless, with the quiet evenings filled with the poignant scent of lilac and laburnums from the gardens, and the nostalgic wild crying of the gulls above the still water.

One morning she learned from Mrs Hocking, the house-keeper, that the girl who helped with the light duties there – such as dusting, arranging flowers and on the general maid's afternoon off, waiting at table – had run off at a moment's notice to Penzance and married a Breton fisherman.

"It's most inconsiderate of her," the kindly Mrs Hocking said. "I've always thought so highly of her, treated her almost as my own daughter. But there! There's no understanding the ways of young things in love."

"Will you get someone else in her place?" Julia asked.

"My dear, yes," the housekeeper said. "But it's finding the right person – not easy in these out-of-the-way places."

Julia thought over what Mrs Hocking had told her. Deborah had been a nice, pretty girl, refined and intelligent to talk to. A wild suggestion came suddenly into her mind – an idea which on second thoughts perhaps was not so wild after all. Why should she not take on the work – or at least, some portion of it – until Mrs Hocking found the person she was looking for? Not for wages, but for keep; surely she could do it, and perhaps John Gauntry would be only too glad to find a temporary way out of the difficulty so easily?

That evening she tentatively put forward the suggestion.

"Don't you see," she said, "I could help you out, if only for the moment? I don't mean that I'd want – that I'd want payment, but – " She broke off, the housekeeper said gently: "But, my dear, 'tisn't the sort of job you'd be doing, not a lady like you. Oh, no, my dear. Unheard of, it would be."

"But, Mrs Hocking," Julia spoke more urgently, "you don't understand. It would *help* me. Help me to stay on here, I mean. It's all rather difficult to explain, but I can't possibly afford to remain much longer. And I've been so happy – at least, happier than I was when I arrived."

"Indeed?" Mrs Hocking regarded her more closely. Then after a pause said slowly, "Well, of course, if you really want me to mention it to Mr Gauntry, I will."

"Oh, *please*," Julia said.

The result of the interview was that Julia, for her services and a small wage, stayed on at the Blue Dolphin while May passed into June and every day seemed to bring more visitors to the little village.

Chapter Eleven

As Julia's duties at the inn were light, she still had a certain amount of leisure time which she filled by walking or reading, and sometimes by taking a jaunt into Penzance where she did some of the shopping for Mrs Hocking. No one could have been kinder to her than the housekeeper and landlord. But as the days passed she begun to realise that this was not enough. At first she'd been content to relax into the peace of life at the Blue Dolphin, anxious only to put her marriage and Stephen behind her. But as her nerves became restored and rested she found herself wondering about the group and about the home she had left. A hundred practical questions began to haunt and disturb her, concerning Stephen in particular – how he was managing, whether he was still at the flat or with Andrea, or whether the Countess had eventually lured him to her own place. She was surprised to find that the thoughts could still so distress her. For the first time she realised acutely that she herself had not behaved well in leaving him so drastically without a word indicating her destination. Yet the idea of writing to him was still distasteful and humiliating to her. She saw that she had indeed burned her boats, and mustering her willpower began to think of her writing as justification for the step she'd taken.

At the beginning of July she'd started work upon a new book, and found surprisingly that it satisfied her, having a maturity neither of the others had possessed.

Then the spell of fine weather gave place to storms; the seas were high, and the flowers in the gardens were dashed and broken by the heavy rains which beat unceasingly from leaden skies. Trelissey had a forlorn aspect, no longer gentle in the gales which swept the waves in monstrous breakers against the rocks and harbour.

One afternoon, feeling she could no longer stay restricted within the inn, Julia, borrowed a mackintosh of Mrs Hocking's and went for a walk along the cliffs. Torrents of rain and spray beat against her face, stinging her cheeks to colour and vitality. But after half a mile she'd had enough and turned upwards to return to the Blue Dolphin by the road which led from the station. There was no one about save the postman in the distance. But as she reached the top of the hill she saw a figure cut into the road from the gates of the station, and heard above the wind the puffing of a train followed by a whistle as it travelled north. Brushing strands of wet hair from her eyes she battled on, then suddenly stopped, staring incredulously ahead. Coming quickly towards her, hatless, loose mackintosh flying and flapping round his long legs, was Stephen.

There was no mistaking him; his walk had the well-remembered swing about it, he was carrying his hat, and a shaft of pale light breaking through the clouds cut clearly across his face. He wasn't smiling, but his attention was rivetted upon her. She saw that, untidy and drenched as she was, he recognised her.

After a second or two she walked on mechanically to meet him, as though it were the most natural thing in the world seeing him there.

"Well," he said, as they met face to face, "you've given me the devil of a time chasing you, Julia."

The commonplace words eased the situation. Yet all she could find to say was, "Oh, Stephen, and you're so wet."

"Not as wet as you," he replied. "I've been in the train. So this is how you spend your time, is it?"

"What do you mean?"

He laughed. "You look like a drowned rat."

"I have to get out sometimes," she replied lamely.

He took her arm, held her there for a moment, kissed her wet hand and said, "You know, Julia, I could certainly beat you. I'm not sure I shouldn't. You deserve it."

A great feeling of relief surged through her. She was

trembling. He wanted her then – he still wanted her.

"Oh, Stephen!" she said. "Oh, Stephen."

"How could you?" he said. "How *could* you do a think like that?" There was no doubting his distress, how shocked he'd been.

"It seemed the only way."

"Hmm! Well, some people have queer ideas." His grip tightened on her arm. "And where is this Blue Dolphin you're hiding in?"

"It's not far," she told him. "But, how on earth did you know?"

"Somebody from Port Todric called in for a drink and saw you there," he said grimly, walking on, "otherwise I should probably still be perusing personal columns in the papers and chasing about the countryside looking for you."

"Oh, Stephen!" she said again.

"Yes, you should be ashamed. Talk about nervous anxiety – it's a wonder I'm not a wreck."

"Well, after all, there *was* some excuse."

"Up to a point," he agreed. "But to run off like that – it was sheer sadism."

"I'm sorry."

"No, you're not," he said, stopping suddenly again and turning her round to face him. "You're not a bit sorry. You're too much of a minx for that. I believe you're glad, Julia. Glad I've had to come trailing after you here, to carry you back. It's true, isn't it?"

She smiled, looking like a child with her wet hair blown in a fringe across her forehead.

"In a way I am. It means that   it means that   perhaps after all we *were* meant to be together."

"Like two drowned rats in a storm. Oh. God, Julia! You *are* the limit!"

She gulped breathlessly as he pulled her along. "There *was* Andrea. I know I was silly, but – "

"Andrea! You've damn' well got to get that bee out of your bonnet. There was nothing in it, ever! Not seriously. Heavens, Julia, you're my *wife*. Couldn't we have talked that out?"

"It didn't seem that we could." She was almost shouting

against the elements. "We always had such awful rows."

"They were partly my fault, I guess," he conceded. "You were alone too much. I'm sorry about it. But *you* should be sorry, too."

"I am."

"Well, that's a change. Now stop the talk and stop your arguing or I'll put you over my knee in a ditch and spank you."

A little later they were back at the inn and Stephen with his usual tact was dealing with Mrs Hocking and Mr Gauntry. Julia, who had gone upstairs, never knew exactly what he said to them, but when she came downstairs they were all looking cheerful, and there was a kindly understanding twinkle in John Gauntry's eyes. Early the next morning they left.

"And don't forget," the landlord said, "any time you feel like a change, just drop a line, and we'll be ready to welcome you."

"You know, Stephen," Julia said later, "they were so kind to me. If only Mrs T was half as nice." She sighed.

"Mrs T is all right," he told her. "Although I think the sick aunt tale has begun to wear a bit thin. I must say she looked after me deuced well – always asking me down to a cup of tea, even offered to darn my socks!"

"Oh, Stephen!"

"Yes, you may well say 'Oh, Stephen'," he said.

"Tell me," Julia said, "who was it recognised me that day?"

"A fellow who makes nets," he answered. "I don't suppose you'd know him. I used to meet him sometimes in the Admiral."

"Oh."

"Yes, a bit surprised he was, too. 'Saw your wife,' he said, 'up at Trelissey. Brought a cup of tea to me.' 'Oh,' I said, 'how was she looking? She's helping a sick aunt up there.' He didn't believe a word, of course, you can't fool a Cornishman. But he pretended to."

Talking over things in this simple manner made Julia wonder however she and Stephen had got into such a mess. The idea in retrospect appeared ludicrous. However far the friendship with Andrea had gone, it was clear now that she had never truly mattered, and Julia had the good sense not to bring the old question up again.

"You see, Stephen," she explained in the train, "I don't mind if I never write another word again – not really – as long as I *matter*. But to be half a wife, and *half* a writer – well, I suppose that didn't seem good enough.'

"You're possessive, with the devil of a temper," he told her. "But you should have known that the group was nothing to me without you." He looked at her closely. "You do realise it, don't you?"

She nodded. "And how did you know," she asked curiously, "that I'd so easily come back with you?"

"My dear, you'd have had no option. I'd have brought you back with me if I'd had to drag you by the hair of the head."

Julia snuggled closer. "Dear Stephen," was all she said.

Their first and only child, a girl, was born in the April of 1906. At an early age it was clear to them that she would have all Stephen's charm and Julia's spirit. They called her Caroline.

Chapter Twelve

By 1913, when Caroline was seven, the Stephen Kerr School was well on its feet, boasting, in the season, from twenty-five to thirty students. Port Todric was now a fashionable haunt for artists and those intelligentsia possessing the means to dabble about with oils and water colours for a season or so, or for as long as the mood took them. Stephen was popular with these people and his work, which was a forerunner of the modern Impressionists, attracted attention by its daring.

By then the Kerrs were established in a house on the hill between Port Todric and Praille. It had been converted from a fisherman's cottage, overlooking both the sea and the moors. Julia loved it; these days perhaps were the happiest of her life. Financial strain had gone. She had managed to write two books in the interim, which though not outstandingly remunerative had at least brought her a measure of notoriety. Even her father had condescended to write to her, and she had once been up to the Midlands at his request to present to him his first grandchild.

They hoped, a little later, to be able to buy their house. Meanwhile, Caroline grew tall and straight, although she was never physically a very strong child. She was fair; fairer than either of her parents, with a wild fey kind of beauty peculiarly her own. She had a quick mind, and with her charm delighted everyone she met, learning at an early age to accept praise and admiration as her due. Sometimes this worried Julia, and the more so because Stephen hopelessly spoiled her.

"She'll grow conceited," she said once. "You shouldn't

give in to her too much, Stephen. She'll expect it always, and become vain and selfish."

He laughed at her. "That little changeling, vain?" he said. "Just look at her. No stockings, no hat – why, she hasn't a vain thought in her head, have you, Carol?"

It was always the same. So Julia gave up remonstrating with him, although she did her best to instil some sort of discipline into the child herself.

Stephen painted her in many ways – in posed portraits, and as a waif on the rocks with her hair blowing and her toes curled among the seaweed. The latter got into the Academy one year, although its technique was criticised in reviews as "outlandish" and "sensational". But Stephen did not care.

"It's good to be talked about," was all he said.

The result of this was that the same summer he was inundated with requests from bored, fashionable women wanting to be portrayed in like manner, which he did without further ado, agreeably supplementing his income.

The Countess had left Port Todric for the South of France in 1907, taking Andrea with her, an event which had caused Julia considerable relief at the time. Since then she had come to accept as a portion of her life the various women who made it their ambition to 'lionise' the attractive and brilliant Stephen Kerr, knowing that he had no deep interest in any of them, and that in any case he was too genuinely fond of herself and Caroline to risk a second time any threat to their life together. He could not help being attractive to women; he might enjoy the knowledge, but it went no further than that. Her anxieties about that were at an end.

Up to the outbreak of war in 1914 it seemed that their ambitions were realised, and that their lives would continue in the pleasant course of the success they had forged together. Then, almost before they were aware of it, the insidious shadows of Europe crept even to the remote far west of Cornwall, and the quiet tempo of existence was disturbed by recruiting campaigns and the continual jingle of 'Pack Up Your Troubles In Your Old Kit Bag' and 'Tipperary'.

It seemed at the beginning absurd for Stephen to think of joining up; the war, they were told, would be over in six months at the least. But the war went on and on.

In the Autumn of 1915, Stephen felt he could stay out of it no longer. Men out of uniform were beginning to be eyed and criticised, especially artists. His pride, as well as his patriotism, was touched.

"It's no good," he said one evening. "I shall have to go." He spoke sombrely, without his usual gaiety.

Julia, looking up from some sewing in her lap, queried sharply: "What do you mean?"

"Join up," he said. "I've been thinking about it for some time, kept putting it off because of you and Carol and the school. But I can't any more. I'm beginning to feel rotten about it all, it's getting on my nerves – the indecision and the feeling I ought to be in it." There was a pause then he went on, "You don't mind – you understand?"

With her voice a little unsteady from the shock, Julia answered slowly "I do mind, of course I do. It will be awful without you. But you must do what you think best. I don't suppose it will be for long, anyhow."

"No, I'm sure," Stephen replied, more at ease now he had told her. "It'll only be for a little while, and you might even be able to carry on for me at the studio whilst I'm away."

"Of course," Julia said, trying to master the dread she felt at Stephen's decision. "I ought easily to do that."

When Caroline heard the news she flung herself with abandon into her father's arms, protesting strongly. "No," she said. "No, you mustn't go, Daddy, you mustn't. You won't be able to paint me any more – I shan't be able to go out with you. You mustn't, *mustn't*!" She was half-sobbing with distress.

"Caroline, stop it," Julia said sharply.

"He'll be killed, I know he will," the girl went on.

"Caroline! How can you say such things?"

"Leave her alone," Stephen said. "Cheer up, Carol, I'll be there and back before you know where you are!"

Later, when she first saw her father in uniform, Carol's enthusiasm was as strong as her opposition had been. This was one of the characteristics in the child that worried Julia – her fluctuating moods of excessive emotion which left her either extremely gay or correspondingly sad. She felt things acutely, but her moods never lasted long.

She is all light and shade, Julia often thought, there's no knowing the real Caroline.

At the beginning of December Stephen went abroad, and upon Julia fell the tasks of running the house and carrying on with the school as best she could. As she had a daily girl to help her now with the cooking and housework, and as, owing to war conditions, the students had dribbled down in numbers to ten, this was not so difficult as it might have been, but she found her hands full and had little time – for which she was grateful – to brood upon Stephen's absence, or indulge in depressing fears.

Three months later he wrote to say that he was expecting leave at any time, and was looking forward to seeing her and Carol again. His letter was buoyant, written in his usual optimistic, breezy style. Julia began to plan and make arrangements for his return.

But he never came.

On March 14th she had a wire which told her with regret that Pt. Stephen Kerr had been killed in action.

For a long time the little piece of paper lay clenched in her fingers; for a long time she stood by the window mechanically staring across the grey sea and sky. The first sound that disturbed her was the lone strange crying of the gulls which forever afterwards was to be linked in her mind with Stephen's death.

Chapter Thirteen

During the weeks following her husband's death, Julia strove to keep her grief to herself for Caroline's sake, doing all that had to be done automatically, referring to Stephen no more than was necessary, so that in time acquaintances no longer openly sympathised or mentioned him to her. But her simulated composure hid a despair few would have guessed. It seemed to her ludicrous and impossible that spring should come to Cornwall, with the opening of the wild thrift and blossom, when Stephen was no longer there to see and share it with her.

Once Caroline had accepted the news, she became quickly reconciled. "I knew he'd be killed," she said. "I told you, Mummy."

"Oh, Caroline, don't," Julia said brokenly.

There was a great deal to be done. Julia had the question of her life and Caroline's now to face. They had saved a certain amount during the last years, but not sufficient to live on the income only; there was also the sentimental aspect of the Stephen Kerr School. For a time she might be able to carry on, in a fashion, but her own speciality was not painting, and she doubted whether she had the flair or capacity to keep it going for long. She faced the possibility of passing it on to someone else, of selling the connection, but hardly knew how to set about it, and when she went into it more thoroughly she found herself resenting the suggestion. After all, it was *Stephen's*. He had striven for it, they had planned and worked it up together. After the energy, the tears, the initiative and time it had cost, it was surely wrong to throw it up so easily.

She was speaking of this one day to Mark Long, one of Stephen's first colleagues with the group. He was still in Port Todric painting hard, and latterly had been assisting Stephen at the studio. The young man's friendship had done something to ease the intolerable loneliness since Stephen's death. She found him sympathetic and understanding without unnecessary sentimentality.

"But why shouldn't I help you out?" he said quickly. "Why not, Mrs Kerr? Stephen and I were friends, and I have the same conception of painting. I suppose we could come to some sort of financial arrangement. When the war ends Port Todric will be popular again. Why not?"

Why not indeed? The more Julia thought about it the more she appreciated the suggestion, and felt that Stephen too would have done so. It seemed the reasonable solution. There was no fear of Mark's being called up, either, since he suffered from trouble with one leg, due to an accident in childhood, and had already been graded as unfit.

And so it was arranged. For a certain percentage of the fees taken, Mark Long agreed to supervise the students for four days of the week.

The new plan was in its initial stages when Richard Benson wrote to his daughter asking her to come home.

I'm becoming an old man, and your step-mother is out a good deal. It would do me good to have you and the child about, and I'm sure you can't want to stick in that godforsaken place now your husband's gone. What about it, Julia – what about coming home again? No reproaches or recriminations mind, on either side. That's all done with. Well, think about it, and let me know.

Your affectionate father,
Richard Benson

Just for a moment she thought of the easy life she would have. The freedom from anxiety and strain tempted her. Then, as quickly, she turned the thought aside, knew it would not do. Why, in a way even, it would be treacherous to Stephen.

She wrote back thanking her father for the offer, but

pointing out that she had made her life in Port Todric, and had besides Stephen's interests to consider.

> Please understand in some ways I should very much like to be with you again, but I just couldn't see the school going under at this point. Stephen put such hard work into it – he had his heart in it, and I want to do now what I think he'd have chosen. However, I'll love to come and stay with you sometimes, and bring Caroline, of course. She's grown a good deal since you saw her, and is very tall for her age.
>
> I hope you understand.
>
> Your affectionate daughter, Julia.

To this she had a reply from her father saying that if she had made up her mind he knew there was no point in trying to dissuade her. However, he said, the matter of Caroline could not lightly be turned aside; she was his only grandchild, and he did not want her to grow up without the advantages she would have had, if Julia had taken a different course.

> In short, I am willing to pay for her to have a good education somewhere – some decent boarding school or other, so that she can fill a proper position in life when she grows up. Also, my dear Julia, though I think you are behaving stupidly in not returning to Linchester, I intend now to continue with the allowance I stopped when you married. Let me know about the school, I have several in mind.

Julia's first reaction, on reading it, was one of irritation and old antagonism. A boarding school! Why should Caroline go to boarding school? Wasn't she capable of bringing up her own child? Really! Her father spoke as though she was of necessity neglecting her daughter's welfare simply because she chose to live in Port Todric rather than Linchester. She was about to reply, turning down the offer impulsively, when doubt swept over her. After all, *had* she a right to stand in the child's way if she herself chose to go? She determined to follow her second idea which was to sound out Caroline on the point in question.

She did so the next day, and to her surprise and dismay Caroline welcomed it with enthusiasm.

"Oh, *do* let me go, Mummy," she cried exuberantly. "I'd love it. Don't you see? I'd meet other girls, and there'd be new things to do – "

Staring hard into her flushed, excited face, Julia asked, "Aren't you happy with me then? I thought you liked Port Todric – you're such a girl for freedom and the open air. Life at school is a very different matter from the way you live here, you know."

"Of course," Caroline agreed, "but I wouldn't mind that – not for a time. Anyhow, Mummy – "

"Yes?"

"Well," Caroline went on, "it hasn't been quite the same since Daddy died. I don't mean I'm not happy with you, but it's been different somehow – not so much fun, and I haven't been able to go to the studio or anything. Besides, I'm tired of Miss Julian's silly school."

"I see," Julia replied, and added after a pause, "Very well, I'll write to your grandfather."

The result of this conversation was that arrangements were made for Caroline to go to school in a country area near Malvern for the autumn term beginning in September. The next few months were not easy ones for Julia. Caroline, sensitive over some matters, was innocently heartless in others, and so concerned with her own affairs that her mother's loneliness did not occur to her. Mother, after all, was Mother – a person to be relied upon, whose business it was to look after one and be there when needed. More and more Julia realised that her earlier fears were justified. Stephen had hopelessly spoiled the child. Perhaps, then, it was better that she *was* going away. A little discipline would not hurt her; obviously when she grew up she would inevitably be spoiled through her looks and charms.

When the time came for her to go, however, Julia had many qualms. She was very young, and there was something pathetic about the sight of her small figure standing in its navy uniform and school hat, by her trunk on the platform. The guard had promised to look after her until Plymouth, where the train would be met by one of the mistresses and some girls going from the district. Despite this Julia had difficulty in restraining herself from taking a ticket and going part of the way with her. But Mark Long, who'd accompanied them, dissuaded her.

"No," he said. "She'll be better on her own. You're a big girl, aren't you, Carol? You'll manage?"

"'Course I will," she promised, smiling bravely, if a little tremulously. She liked and admired Mark, and he was very fond of her.

"Julia," he said afterwards, once the goodbyes and tears were over, and the train steamed away, "she's got spirit, that little thing. And she's going to be a beauty."

He always called her Julia now.

"I know. That's what troubles me."

"Troubles you – what on earth for? You should be glad!"

"She lacks balance and stamina and she's very headstrong. I wonder what lies ahead for her."

"So is her mother very headstrong," Mark said with a smile, "that's no handicap."

"Her mother isn't a beauty. Besides, Mark, things are changing. Values are changing – the war is doing something to the world."

"Oh, come now, this isn't like you. Generally you're so optimistic."

She sighed. "I expect I'm just drained. First Stephen, now Caroline."

"Yes, but it isn't as if you aren't deep down a self-contained person," he said thoughtfully. "I'm not sure that this isn't the best thing for you. Not Stephen's death, of course – but Caroline's going away. You weren't made just to dote on a child. You're a being, apart from a woman. Maybe you haven't realised that sufficiently before, and now life's taking a hand. I suppose that's what existence is, really, finding oneself, time after time."

They walked on.

"Perhaps you're right," she said.

Once she'd grown accustomed to Caroline's absence it appeared Mark might be right. She seemed to take on a new spurt of energy and initiative. She was free to go down more to the studio, and the relinquishing of maternal worries made her feel and look younger. Getting out more helped to ease the ache of Stephen's death. The less she was in the house, she found, the better she felt; and at the studio something of Stephen seemed to linger, encouraging and working with her.

After the first pangs of homesickness, Caroline started to enjoy certain aspects of boarding school life. Her looks and bright manner made her a favourite alike with girls and staff, which was no mean achievement. The restraints of having to walk in a crocodile, of punctuality at meal times, of never going out without gloves, and the hundred and one other minor impositions, annoyed her. But on the other hand there were the joys of midnight feasts and the dancing class, which she loved. It was nice also to talk about her father to the girls, who had been, she told them, 'a very famous man – a great artist and brave soldier'.

Even her favourite schoolmistress, Miss Horn, who took drill, was interested in her anecdotes concerning the Port Todric artists. There was an advantage, Caroline found, in being the daughter of one, and having a mother who wrote.

Caroline stayed at Malvern for seven years, until she was seventeen, dividing her holidays between her grandfather and Julia.

Richard Benson died in 1921, three years after the war had ended, leaving half his fortune to his wife, and half to Caroline, the capital to be held in trust for her until she became twenty-one, the income to be Julia's meanwhile. If, before that Caroline died, leaving any children, the sum was to be theirs under similar conditions. Otherwise it reverted to Julia. Out of this Julia herself was to receive a limited income for life. But it was not large. Her father's fortune had diminished during recent years, and he did not leave so much as had been expected – thirty thousand when death duties and minor bequests had been cleared. Still, Caroline's share meant that she could be independent for life, and that Julia would never be reduced to penury.

When Caroline returned Julia felt almost a stranger to the elegant, polished young woman who spoke with such ease and assurance on topics quite alien to her mother. She was tall, half a head taller than Julia, and had fulfilled all former expectations of beauty. Her skin had not lost its wild rose freshness and radiance, her hair, of a soft dull gold, rippled from a forehead that was wide and clear above darkly lashed grey eyes. Yet there was something restless about her – something which Julia soon sensed, beyond the assumed remoteness and poise.

For the first week or so the future was not discussed, but after that Julia brought up the topic.

"Have you thought what you want to do, darling?" she queried. "Work, I mean – a career?"

Caroline looked surprised. "No, why should I? I mean, there's no *need* exactly, is there? Not with Grandpa's money coming to me, and – and – well, I've only just got home, I'd like a bit of fun."

"Of course," Julia said. "But it's a good feeling to have an interest, and to be independent – *really* independent. I mean, relying on oneself entirely."

"Were you?" Caroline enquired bluntly.

Julia flushed. "I meant to be," she answered. "I fought for it and was halfway there; and when I married I gave up all the security I'd had from my father."

"Didn't you ever regret it?" Caroline asked.

"No," Julia answered honestly, "I didn't."

"Still," went on Caroline, "there's no *need* for me to. It makes a difference."

"We shan't be *terribly* well off, you know," Julia went on after a pause. "There's still four years before you're twenty-one, and the studio is not bringing in much at the moment. You won't be able to have the extravagances you've been used to at boarding school."

Caroline frowned. "Oh, Mummy, you sound so dreary. Do you mean you want me to go into a shop or something? Because I couldn't, I just *couldn't*."

"Of course I didn't mean that," Julia said sharply, "but I think it would be better for you to have some interest."

"I've lots of interests," Caroline said. "Mark's promised to take me sketching one afternoon when he's not at the studio, like Daddy used to. You won't mind, will you?"

There was something challenging in the girl's tone which Julia did not like.

"What do you mean, Caroline? Mark's an old friend. Why should I object to him?"

Caroline shrugged her shoulders. "I don't know, but since I've come back all I do or say seems to be wrong."

Julia sighed.

"You're being rather childish and quite mistaken. I'm afraid boarding school has put a lot of silly ideas into your head."

To keep her occupied, Julia encouraged Caroline in her visits to the studio, where Mark did his best to get her started with drawing, and water colour. But Caroline showed no real initiative. She had quickness and a facile capacity for copying but little originality, and was quickly bored.

"Oh," she said one day, flinging down her pencil and rubber, "I'm tired of this old drawing board. Let's go out, Mark. Come with me to the rocks – I want to dabble my toes and shake my hair in the sun."

She smiled at him, radiant.

"I can't, Carol, there are the students."

"Oh, bother the students! Who cares?" She knew she was tantalising him, but his refusal to concede to her whims only encouraged her admiration and secret regard for him.

Once she said to Julia, "You know, Mummy, Mark's awfully attractive; not in the Rudolf Valentino-ish way, but – stronger, Clive Brook-ish."

Julia laughed. "I see you're film struck."

"No, I'm not!" Caroline spoke crossly. "How silly you make everything sound."

"Not silly, funny," Julia remarked. "I suppose I do rather see the comical side. My books are like that."

"If you write I suppose it's different," Caroline pointed out shrewdly. "You can get things out of your system. But it's different when you're a person like me."

"How different?"

"Oh, well, you see, I've got a lot inside of me I can't show," Caroline confided. "I'm really rather serious and – and restless underneath. I want things dreadfully."

"What things, Caroline?"

"Oh, unexplainable things. I don't know – beautiful things. I want them to last for ever and ever. Never to die. But they can't, and I know they can't, and that makes me unhappy sometimes."

"Caroline, darling – "

"Oh, don't be sloppy, Mother. It's nothing to be sad about. But I can't just be contented like you and placid all the time."

Placid? Julia smiled ironically, recalling certain moments in her life with Stephen.

"Well," she said, "don't get too concerned and wrapped up in yourself, it's not good for you."

As time went on it seemed that her daughter was growing further away from her, and Julia began to realise acutely that Caroline was growing up in a world that had not existed before the war, a world of cocktails, slang, and uncertain morality which had been only faintly foreshadowed in occasional individuals like the Countess. Caroline herself, though not yet eighteen, was already becoming caught up into the tempo of the period. She bought a new gramophone record and was forever dancing to it or humming in her bedroom a strange new tune called "Dardanella"; she got to know a girl called Muriel Lane who lived between Praille and Penzance and asked Caroline to parties to which Julia did not like to refuse permission. The climax came, however, when she returned one night by car, in the company of a young man, with the excuse she'd missed the bus, so Alex had been perfectly sweet and given her a lift. This may have been true, but Julia saw that the girl was 'all in', and had besides been drinking.

The parties stopped for Caroline. But her restlessness went on. Julia was at her wits' end to know what to do with her.

Then, shortly after her eighteenth birthday, Caroline told her that she and Mark were in love with each other and wanted to be engaged.

Julia was astounded. She'd accepted their friendship, but that there could be anything else between a girl like Caroline and a man old enough to be her father seemed quite incredible.

She tried to laugh it off.

"Oh, come now, darling, I know Mark's a dear, and quite

distinguished and clever in his way, but in love with him! Why, he's twenty years older than you."

"That doesn't matter." Caroline spoke stubbornly. "Nothing could make any difference, Mummy. I love him and we're going to get married."

"I see." Julia's voice was hard. "And how long has Mark been feeling like this? Since I suppose he *must* reciprocate?"

"Oh, ages," Caroline said lightly, "but he fought against it, because he didn't think I knew my own mind, and because of age and his leg and everything."

After a pause Julia pointed out slowly, "I suppose you realise, Caroline, that young girls like you quite often have this sort of feeling for a man much older, and then find in time that it's worn off, that it was just a phase?"

It was the worst thing she could have said, and a moment later she knew it.

"I knew you'd say that," Caroline cried tempestuously. "It's always the same. You never take me seriously. But I *am* serious this time, I *am*, and whatever you think won't make any difference. Nothing will."

"You're under age. I can forbid you getting married, you understand that?" Julia queried coldly.

"If you did I'd wait," Caroline stated, "and I'd never forgive you for wasting time Mark and I could have had together."

"Caroline, stop it!" Julia said, upset. "You'd better go to your room and calm down. I shall see Mark about this myself."

"You won't make him stop loving me," Caroline cried, as she rushed to the door. "Whatever you say, you won't do that. I *told* him you'd kick up hell."

The door banged, leaving Julia sitting white-faced on the chair by the window. To speak like that to her! Caroline, her daughter and Stephen's. It seemed unbelievable. She put her hand to her head and found she was shaking. If only she had Stephen to help her out now. How would he have tackled the problem?

She saw Mark that same day. He was shamefaced, apologetic, but confirmed what Caroline had told her.

"I've tried to stop it," he said. "I've pointed out that I'm a middle-aged man who can give her very little of the things she's entitled to. But Caroline knows her own mind, Julia, and – "

"And you love her?"

"I'm – I adore her."

Julia moistened her lips with her tongue. "I see. So it looks as though I'm up against a brick wall, doesn't it?"

Mark suddenly looked tired.

"Oh, don't talk like that. I know what you must feel. I'm a contemporary of Stephen's, and lame into the bargain."

Julia laughed harshly. "Oh, *that*. Do you think that sort of thing worries me? Listen, Mark," she went on in a softer, kinder voice, "you must believe me, it isn't only Caroline I'm thinking of – indeed, it's odd, I'm not sure that she *does* bother me so much after all, although she's my daughter. We've never been very close, I have always felt she was Stephen's child more than mine, and since she came back from boarding school it's been worse. No. It's you."

"Me?"

"I don't think you realise what marriage with Caroline would mean. Perhaps I shouldn't say it – but she's selfish, Mark, and after all she *is* terribly young. How would you cope with a young restless thing whose very values are completely different from those of our generation? Don't you see? She's not found herself yet, doesn't really know the first thing about herself. And another thing, Mark, if she tired of you do you imagine she'd have any scruples in throwing it all up?" She broke off, a wild, sudden colour in her cheeks. He admired her courage and spirit, and wished that it was she he could have loved.

"You're a little hard," he said.

"No, I'm facing up to the truth."

"Look here, Julia," he began again after a pause, awkwardly, "do you want me to go away or something? Shall I pack up and disappear for six months? If you like I'm willing to do that, give Caroline time to find out whether she really knows her own mind or not."

She shook her head. "No. It would be no good. I know my daughter. Once she's set her heart on a thing nothing on earth will change her. Unless, of course, I *had* hoped – " Julia faltered " – that you might of your own initiative consider not going on with it?" She broke off, aware from his expression this was a vain hope.

Mark smiled wrily. "But I've told you – I love her," he reaffirmed simply, as though there were nothing more to be said on the matter.

"I see. Well, in that case – "

"I know what you must feel," he said, more bitterly. "You resent the idea."

"I don't resent it. She's my child, though, and naturally I don't wish to see her going headlong into unhappiness."

"Thank you."

"Because I'm afraid that's what it will be," she continued, "for both of you. And there is the group, too. That matters."

"But, Julia, I shall still be able to carry on there."

"Well, I hope so," she said. "But Caroline is possessive, she shouldn't marry an artist."

"Why?"

"Because an artist – or a part of him, if he's serious – must be free," Julia told him. "That was the lesson I had to learn in my life with Stephen, and not without some tears. And I'm very different from Caroline. Stronger, more able to steer my own course."

He sighed. "Well, I'm sorry. But you see how things are. I *have* offered to go away. I don't see what other suggestion there is."

"Except marriage."

"Yes, except marriage."

There was a long pause, in which she moved away and stood with her back to him, facing the window. Then she turned round and said, "Very well, if that's how you feel, Mark."

"Do you mean – ?"

"I shan't fight you for ever," she said. "Why should I? But I shall expect you to give her time."

"Of course."

"And not to be too shocked," she went on, "if she *does* change. She may, you know, once the opposition's gone. But, of course, that's your responsibility."

So the interview ended, Mark conscious that he'd

displeased and worried Julia, she aware that her friendship had not been sufficient, nor would be, to divert his passion from marriage with Caroline.

As the weeks passed, however, she began to wonder if, after all, everything had not worked out for the best. Seeing that she had won her point, Caroline became more amenable and thoughtful and seemed so happy, so apparently wrapped up in Mark, that Julia began to feel her own apprehensions had been misplaced, and that they might find happiness together.

"You really ought to be pleased," Caroline remarked one day. "I'm sure Daddy would. He liked Mark, and we shall be able to carry on the school together."

"You'll be able to help him, I hope," Julia said, ignoring Caroline's thoughtless reference to the school, ill-timed since she had no idea herself of giving up the reins until age or circumstance forced her, which should not be for some time yet.

The next few months were spent in a whirl of preparation and plans for the wedding. There seemed no point in delaying the matter long, and once she had reconciled herself to the idea Julia strangely enough found herself looking forward to the time when the responsibility of her daughter would be diverted to other shoulders. She would have time at last – a thing that had never yet been hers – to get down to her own work in peace, the richer for experience, a fuller fund of knowledge to give to whatever small public was hers.

Because I *can* write, she said to herself with conviction, and I'm not really old yet.

Old? The face which confronted her in the glass was still young. At that moment she did not look her forty years; her mouth was relaxed in a half smile, her eyes eager again with thoughts which had lain dormant for a long time. There was still no trace of grey in her hair. She was erect and slim, and new ideas already swarmed in her mind. Perhaps even yet a great deal that was good in life lay in wait for her.

After a period of house hunting, one was found for Caroline a mile from Julia's on the main road to Praille, a charming cottage with which she fell in love instantly. Julia thought it rather a long way from the town, needing as well a good many repairs, but the rent was not too high, and Mark liked it. He had an income of his own, sufficient to include the running of a small car which Caroline insisted upon learning to drive. So the months slipped by, warm summer months, until, on a clear windless day in October, Mark and Caroline were married at the Port Todric parish church.

Caroline, in the white bridal gown and veil, could not have looked lovelier. There was a full congregation at the church, which included a large proportion of artists. Months later the bride was painted in her wedding. dress by Sir Geoffrey Wilkes, an event which gave her considerable pleasure. After the ceremony the newly-married couple went for a few weeks to Italy, and when they returned the seas were wild and high again round Port Todric, the evenings filled with the sound of wind and thin high crying of the gulls.

Julia had a fire burning in the cottage, with tea already laid. Caroline ran to the blaze eagerly.

"Oh," she cried, "it's so cold here. Thank heaven for a fire. I feel like a cocktail. Do you, Mark?"

"Cocktails?" echoed Julia. "But I haven't got drinks in for you."

"What? No drinks? Oh, Mummy!" Caroline made a moue. "Never mind, Mark's got whisky in his bag."

"Caroline! *Whisky*? But that's not – not *you*!"

Caroline laughed. "Why not? Darling! Don't be old-fashioned."

Mark went upstairs, and after a pause Caroline continued, "What a horrible noise those birds make. Ugh! Like ghosts shrieking – banshees."

"You're tired, and it's getting dark," Julia said. "You won't notice them in the morning."

But Caroline doesn't really belong here, she thought. She never has. She's alien. She's of a world I do not know. Can she really be *my* child?

Then Mark returned with the whisky.

"Here you are, darling, do you good." He looked at her anxiously. "Still cold?"

She shook her head. "Not terribly."

He's going to spoil her, Julia thought. She has him by the little finger.

During the next week or two this fact became the more apparent. Julia did her best to shut her eyes to it; if they were happy that was the main thing. And at the moment Caroline seemed content. There was really no reason why she shouldn't be, Julia decided with faint irony, recalling the hard financial struggle she and Stephen had had in the beginning. She had a daily girl to help her, and was free to be with Mark at the studio most of the day if she wished. All the same an intangible fear lay at the back of Julia's mind, something she couldn't exactly define but which had its roots in Caroline's excessive exuberance and in Mark's complete enslavement.

During the winter several students left again, but in the following spring there was a rush of visitors to Port Todric, and the studio was filled to overcrowding. Julia arranged an exhibition of Stephen's work at the Gallery, which was received enthusiastically by the critics. His colourful impressionistic style was now quite in vogue, and two of his war paintings were purchased by London galleries. A new trend of painting – surrealism – had come vividly to life, with the post-war period of jazz and changing values. There was an influx of these new disciples to Port Todric – cynical, colourful young people who made an attempt to revolutionise the Stephen Kerr School. But Julia, keeping her head, would have none of it.

"This is not the kind of work Stephen would have liked," she said to Mark. "He was modern, unconventional, yes; but Stephen could *draw*. He took his work seriously. These can't. We don't want them associated with us."

"Some are all right," Mark temporised. "You can't keep the clock static."

"No, but we must keep a sense of proportion," she said. "They can come to the school so long as they're willing to learn. But we mustn't be used as advertisement for a fashion that has no real roots or values."

"I don't see how we're going to differentiate. And if they can pay . . ."

"I think we must establish something – some certificate or other which can be given on leaving to any student who's reached the standard set by the group," Julia suggested, ruminating. "Say, the Stephen Kerr Certificate, labelling the holder as an Associate."

"But would that count for much, out of Cornwall?"

"It would safeguard us," Julia replied promptly, "and in a sense it would advertise us."

Mark stared at her admiringly. Funny what a business head she had, this bright-eyed little woman, the mother of his Caroline.

"Very well," he agreed. And so the Stephen Kerr certificate was inaugurated. By the end of the summer Julia took on an adjoining room, and a little later had the two studios converted into one. In September there were thirty-five students working there.

Chapter Fourteen

For the first year of her married life, Caroline was completely happy, absorbed by the novelty and Mark's passion for her, although the physical side seemed to her something of a bore, a troublesome detail to be got over as quickly as possible then forgotten. But her coldness in this respect was well concealed, and Mark was content, never ceasing to wonder that this lovely girl should belong to him, should have come to care for him. It was true that the domestic side was uncongenial to her – she never attempted to hide it. But he was so much in love with her that he did not allow the fact to worry him, and, due to the help they had, the wheels of the household ran comparatively smoothly and he had little to complain of. As time went by, however, she showed an increasing tendency to extravagance which, in the end, he was forced to point out to her.

"We just can't do it, darling," he said one day. "All the parties, I mean, and the meals out. It isn't that I grudge you anything, Carol, all I have is yours, and you know it. But – well, the car alone costs money, and I'm not exactly a rich man."

"But, *darling*," Caroline protested, "I don't really spend so awfully much, and you like me to have nice perfume and things, don't you, Mark? You wouldn't like me to dress like a drab, would you? And anyhow, it isn't as if I haven't got money of my own. And when I'm twenty-one there'll be lots more. We're not *poor*."

"I now, but – " Mark looked worried. "Oh, hang it all, Caroline, I want to feel that I can keep my own wife. I don't want to have to depend on your capital."

She pouted. "That's just silly. What difference does it make? You mustn't be old-fashioned. Think how awful it would be if I just went dull and plain with thick stockings and lanky hair! You wouldn't love me any more, now would you?"

"Yes, I would," he declared. "I'd love you anyhow. And you'd never grow dull and plain, Caroline, you couldn't. But — "

"But what?"

"Well," he said slowly, taking the bull by the horns, "I think perhaps our pleasures could be simpler."

"What do you mean by simpler?" she spoke sharply.

"We're not together very much, are we? Not properly alone, I mean!"

She laughed. "Really, Mark! You are funny. We must have friends. You wouldn't want me to sit by the fire all night holding your hand, would you?"

The blunt words shook him, revealing a side of her he'd not seen before.

"There's no need to speak like that," he said shortly.

"I'm sorry, but you shouldn't be so stuffy," she said, pouting again.

She looked so like a child rebuked that he softened instantly. "Darling! we mustn't act like this."

The small difference passed off, but the sting of it remained, and Caroline seemed quicker to take offence, a little more restless and anxious to have her own excitements and pleasures. Mark, on his side, began to feel at times oddly tired and jarred. However much he loved Caroline, there was a certain strain in keeping up with her quick change of moods and emotional demands. Sometimes, when he did not kiss her or make sufficient fuss of her, she would say impatiently, "Oh! I think you're bored – I think you're just getting used to me. I hate being a *habit*."

At others, when he tried to take her in his arms, she would contrarily push him away and exclaim, "Oh, Mark, don't be sloppy. Look, you've untidied my hair!"

Afterwards she generally had the grace to repent, telling him she was sorry, she *did* so love him, only . . .

"Only what, Caroline?" he asked once, wearily.

"I don't know. I don't think I'm a very nice person," she admitted. "I get restless and don't know why, Mark. I wish I did. I'd rather be good like you and my mother. But something makes me say horrid things. I don't really mean them, you know. I expect I've got a complex or something. Freud would know."

Her statement struck him as extraordinarily naive.

"Carol," he said, "you're so funny. Why Freud?"

"The psychologist, darling. He knows all about women like me."

"How do *you* know?"

"That young man you introduced me to – David Blair – was explaining it all," Caroline told him.

Mark looked puzzled. Blair was a young tutor of economics down from the Midlands for the summer vacation, and since talking to him with Caroline at the studio some days ago, Mark was unaware they'd met again.

"But when did you have this pow-wow?" he queried, curious.

"Yesterday," she said. "We met in the Blue Cat, and had a coffee. Quite by chance, of course, but it was rather fun."

"Hmm."

Mark said no more, but he was discomfited. He didn't care for Blair, who was far too slick and charming and assured for his liking. And now this psychology stunt! Typical, he thought – the obvious technique he *would* use with an impressionable young woman. However, the matter seemed too trivial to worry about so he put it out of his mind and was surprised amd mildly aanoyed a week later when Carol told him after their evening meal one night that she had asked Blair for coffee on the Tuesday evening.

"But why? What did you want to do that for?"

"Surely you're not annoyed?" she said quickly. "I thought you liked him."

"Darling, I'm sure you didn't," Mark said. "Speak the truth. Oh, I suppose he's all right, but hardly my sort of fellow."

"Is that any reason why he shouldn't come to coffee? I like him anyway. He's amusing."

"Oh, yes, he can *talk*!" Mark admitted. "And since you've asked him I'll have to put up with it, I suppose."

There was a little pause, then Caroline remarked, "After all, it's good to have someone young in occasionally."

"Aren't you happy with what we have?" Mark asked slowly.

"Of *course* I am. Only – well – it's nice sometimes just to have *fun*."

What a child she sounded. What a child she really was, Mark reminded himself, looking at her. For all her pretended sophistication she was only twenty – half his age. He sighed, caught her to him, and held her head against his breast, stroking her hair. She did not withdraw. After a moment she asked softly, "Mark, what is it? Why don't you say something. What's the matter?"

"I don't know. You make me wish – "

"Well, what do I make you wish?"

"Oh, unobtainable things, love. Sometimes I feel it's an illusion, all this – that we're in some dream you and I – some impossible beautiful illusion that's going to fade. I want to hold you to me, and I can't. I *can't!*"

"Mark!" She was disturbed in spite of herself. "How funny to hear you talk like that. Are you all right – *are* you?"

He realised that she didn't understand. "Quite all right," he said with forced gaiety. "Take no notice of me. Just a mood of mine, like yours, darling."

"No, my moods are different. We're really not a bit alike. That's probably why we got married. Opposites, you know."

"And did Freud say that too?"

"Oh, I guess he knew all about it," she agreed. "Like God."

"So you *do* believe in God!"

"I'm not sure," she admitted. "No – I don't think I do, not really, not your kind, not the moral fatherly God. I wish I did, I think life would be much easier."

He was not sure whether to laugh or take her seriously. So he just said, "Why?"

"Because it would be something to hang on to," she said, with a shrug of her shoulders. "I haven't anything, you see, so I mustn't think too deeply. I'd get frightened."

"But, Caroline, you've got *me*. You've got my love."

"Oh, I know, darling, but – you might *stop* loving me, or – or anything might happen – "

"You mean you might stop loving *me*?" he said.

"It might happen either way," she admitted.

"Oh, Caroline."

"It's no good being sentimental," she said, "and coming a flop, is it?"

He stared at her incredulously. "I wonder if you realise how completely cruel you can be, Caroline?"

"Of course I do," she said lightly, gaily. "I was just teasing. I should always love you, Mark, because I admire you, you see."

"Admire?"

She nodded. "You're so detached, somehow, and above everything that disturbs and worries other people."

"Such as?"

"Ah, never mind." She laughed and went to the window.

"Let's go out for a walk," she said, "on to the beach. Let's take our shoes off and run on the sands."

His doubts left him suddenly. She was adorable in this mood.

"Right," he said. "We'll go to the point."

He felt young, at ease again. When she looked and behaved like that, she could do with him what she wanted. Nothing else counted in comparison. Nothing at all.

Chapter Fifteen

Julia's fourth book was published at the end of 1926. It was the story of the eternal struggle between a woman's love and her career, and because it had the genuine stamp of truth about it, and because she had been free to write it unrestricted by worry or other ties, it caught the public fancy, and was soon running into a second impression. It was a theme which suited the era of feminine emancipation and the publishers were delighted. She had now considerable royalties coming in, which, for the first time since her marriage, enabled her to spend money without undue consideration for the future. She was not a rich woman, her income from her father had been badly cut by falling share prices, but knowledge of her independence was a sweet thing to her, and except for a certain loneliness she was happy.

She had become a favourite now with the fishing people and natives who had at last ceased to regard her as a "foreigner". Occasionally she gave tea parties for some of the old people, which brought her as much genuine pleasure as her guests. Mrs Tremayne was over seventy now, and no longer let the rooms where Julia and Stephen had first started their married life. She had a niece living there, who helped her out when necessary, and who, with Mrs T herself, frequently called on Julia.

It was from her, one afternoon, that Julia heard the disquieting news about Caroline.

"Of course," her ex-landlady was saying, sitting primly upright in the best black silk coat she had worn on special occasions for the last twenty years, "tedn't my business, but I do think that husband of Miss Caroline's should be taking more care of the friends she do take up with."

"But, Mrs Tremayne," Julia protested, "I'm sure Mark – my son-in-law – knows all about Caroline's acquaintances. And you must realise that my daughter is a good deal younger than he is. She needs young people about her sometimes."

Mrs T sniffed. "That may be. There are young people and young people, Mrs Kerr. And a lot of 'em I cannot abide nowadays. Why, if they'd gone on in my young days as *that* young fellow goes on, they'd have been thrown out – thrown out of Port Todric, or my name's not Sarah Tremayne."

Looking confused and worried, Julia said, "But I don't understand – *what* young fellow?"

"The professor, as they call him," Mrs Tremayne explained, "the one in the red shirt who was down in the summer. Always out with her then he was, but now it's worse. Of course, as I've said, tedn't my business. But you being a friend of mine, and knowing what folks be, I thought it my duty to say a word, just so maybe you'd speak to her."

"I'm quite sure," Julia said a trifle coldly, "that my son-in-law is well aware of his wife's friendships, so I don't really think there's any need to worry about it. And now, let me give you a cup of tea."

Nothing more was said on the matter. But afterwards Julia wished she'd asked Mrs Tremayne to explain more fully – to clarify her statements concerning Caroline and young Blair. She recognised Blair was the man referred to. He'd come down for the Christmas break; she herself had seen him talking to Caroline on the harbour a few days earlier. All the same, the suggestion that there could be anything more than friendship in the affair was absurd. Or was it? Looking back she admitted to herself certain aspects which had seemed to her entirely negligible before – a look of strain and tension about Mark's eyes recently, an added glow and excitement about Caroline, together with an apparent boredom over household affairs. She was out more, and seemed disinclined to discuss anything with her. Her head seemed filled with ridiculous ideas of psychology and strange modern poetry concerned with repressions and sex. What did it all mean? Julia sighed. She'd speak to her daughter. She did not like the idea, but felt it was her duty.

Caroline, when tackled, was both indignant and evasive.

"You've been listening to gossip," she said angrily. "I can't understand you. You know what these people are, yet when some old busybody comes whispering in your ear, you take it all in. It's ridiculous."

"All the same," Julia persisted, "you *are* a married woman, dear, and it isn't fair to Mark to give the busybodies, as you call them, a chance."

"Fair to *Mark*! And what about fairness to *me*?" Caroline asked sharply. "Is my life to be ordered by these people and the filthy lies they put about? Well, I can tell you, it isn't. And if I choose to be friendly with David I shall be. I need *some* recreation, in all conscience. Do you realise that my life isn't exactly all fun with Mark so wrapped up in the school as he is? Sometimes I think he's far more interested in the group than in me. I'm not sure he shouldn't have married *you*. You have the same interests."

Julia flushed. "Caroline! How can you say such things?"

Caroline stuffed her handkerchief to her eyes and burst into a storm of weeping. "Oh, it's stupid. So petty. I feel awful. I don't know what's the matter with me. I'm not sleeping at all. I just don't know."

Julia shook her head. She was worried. Presently she said, "I'll make you a cup of something to drink. You seem very on edge. Have you been to the doctor recently?"

Caroline shook her head. "No, I'm not ill. But mother – "

"Yes?"

"Could you perhaps – have you any sherry?"

Julia looked doubtful. "Wouldn't tea be better? Aren't you taking too much sherry these days? It isn't good you know, Caroline."

"Oh, *another* lecture! All right, *tea*."

But Julia gave her the sherry.

Caroline's outburst had left her mother more worried than angry. She blamed herself for not having realised earlier that all was not well with her daughter. And what was the reason? What was wrong? Unhappiness with Mark? Was she really getting entangled with this young man Blair, or could it be that she was going to have a child?

She broached the matter from the health angle to Mark the following day.

"Caroline seems a little run down," she said tentatively. "Do you think it might be a good idea to go away for Christmas?"

He shook his head. "I suggested it, but she wouldn't."

"But why?"

"Oh, she's arranged one or two parties," he said impatiently. "Boring affairs to me, but they seem to be Caroline's life."

Julia was silent for a few moments, then she said seriously, "Caroline hasn't enough to do. You've spoiled her, Mark, as Stephen did. If you value your happiness, see to it."

He looked up sharply. "What do you mean?"

"Get rid of the girl," she said. "Let Caroline do a few of the things she took on when she married you. She's your wife. Yet you allow her to neglect the house and go chasing about the countryside with some dilettante who's doing her no good – or you."

She expected a denial from him, some sharp rejoinder. But it did not come. Instead he said dully, "I see. So you know."

"*Mark*! You admit it. It's true?"

He shrugged his shoulders. "My eyes aren't shut. I'm not entirely without imagination."

"Then why on earth didn't you – ?"

"Stop it?" he queried bitterly. "Have you ever tried to stop Caroline doing anything she wanted to? Besides, there's nothing concrete. Most of it's – well, my own instinct."

"Of what?"

"She's bored with me."

"And you're content to let it go like that?" Julia cried impatiently. "Just to wait and watch while she – while she – "

"It will pass," he said. "It's only a phase. She's fascinated, and you can hardly blame her – a middle-aged man like me, and a young attractive fellow."

"Oh!" she burst out. "You're impossible. I can't understand you."

He turned away from her, and when he looked at her again she saw his face was white, almost deathly.

"Love isn't always possessive," he said quietly.

"It must be, with some people, if it's to endure at all."

She left him with the unhappy satisfaction that although her talk had done little practical good, at least the matter had been brought into the daylight. They all knew where they were.

Christmas came and went, followed by a spring which, to Mark, was filled with an unhappy tension, kept alive always by the knowledge that Blair was to return for Easter. His name now was seldom mentioned by either of them, Caroline guiltily aware that her husband was put on edge by it. With the existing strain between them her thoughts instinctively turned more and more towards David. The affair had gone further than either Julia or Mark suspected. She knew now that she was in love with him, and had been from the very beginning, just as she was aware of the mistake she'd made in marrying Mark. He was clever, of course, and good, and she cared for him very much in a certain way, but not in the right way for marriage. Her whole being now was aflame with a bitter repressed passion which made her body rigid and filled her mind with but one thought: David, David! Yet when he was with her he was not really kind to her. In Blair's character there was none of that reverence for her beauty which had been so easy to stir in most men. He desired her body, as he had desired other women's, but her character he saw through and mildly despised.

But if I were free, she often thought, now knowing defeat, it would be different. It's because I'm married he can be so cruel. If I were free he would marry me.

And so she deceived herself, letting go conscience, all former ties, and regard for Mark. No longer troubling to keep up a pretence of being in love with him. Like most cold women she had the faculty for being roused by just one type of man, and David Blair happened to be that type: ruthless, brilliant, and fundamentally amoral. Shortly before he returned at Easter, she became buoyed up again and sang about the house while her eyes shone and an excited flush stained her cheeks. Mark meanwhile watched her with a dull aching unhappiness that gnawed away at him inside until there were times when he looked almost an old man.

Julia, seeing this, tried once more to pull things together. "It's no good your going on like this," she said abruptly one day. "You're killing yourself, and letting Caroline mess up her life."

"What can I do?"

Julia decided to be brutal. "If you can't put your foot down," she said, "it might be better to free Caroline."

"What?" he gasped. "Do you mean divorce?"

"Why not? It would be better than living as you do."

"I shouldn't dream of it," he said decisively. "This will pass. Besides, it's not as serious as you think."

However, on the day before David's arrival, he spoke to her. She was placing some flowers in a Lalique bowl on the table. All was clear restful blue about the room, from the patterned linen curtains to the upholstery and hand-painted standard lamp by the fireplace. Caroline was wearing a simple blue woollen frock with a hint of mauve at the neck and cuffs. The sun fell on her soft hair, lighting it to pale gold. He had never seen her looking lovelier. For some moments he watched her without speaking. Then he said to her, "Caroline?"

"Yes?"

"I want to talk to you."

She spoke shortly. "Oh, well. What is it?"

"Please look at me."

She did so, with her eyebrows raised.

"Thank you. I know very well that you have not much interest in me or my feelings," he continued, "but all the same, I do ask you to have a little thought for me from now on."

"Just exactly what do you mean, Mark?"

"Blair," he said, forcing the issue. "I don't want him round here when he returns."

Her colour deepened. "Very well. You've always made that rather obvious. I'll see he doesn't worry you."

"And not only that – I think it would be better if you two didn't meet either."

She laughed. "Don't be ridiculous. You sound mid-Victorian."

"Perhaps I am. There are worse things. The point is we do

102

happen to be married, and for a long time things have been going wrong between us. Caroline, surely it's worth an effort?"

"What?" She spoke lifelessly.

"Oh – all we've had together," he said with feeling. "We used to be happy. You cared for me then. Can't we at least give it a chance?"

"It's *had* a chance," she said coldly. "I'm sorry if you're not happy. It's not entirely my fault. I tried at first, but – "

"But what?"

"Oh, Mark, what's the *use* of talking about it. I suppose I shouldn't have married you, but sometimes people make mistakes."

"I see. So it *was* mistake. You wish now, I suppose, that you were free to marry Blair?"

She did not reply.

"Well, can't you speak?"

When still she said nothing, he took her by the shoulders, controlling with difficulty an impulse to shake her.

"*Caroline*! Did you hear what I said?"

"Let me go," she cried, so wildly he immediately released her. Then, defiantly, with sullen cruelty, she answered, "Yes, if you must know – yes, I *do* wish I were free. There, are you satisfied?"

There was a brief pause before he replied bitterly, "And do you suppose he'd want you if you were?"

"How can you think he wouldn't? That's a rotten thing to suggest."

He laughed. "He *might* of course. You'll have money soon."

Caroline, a shade paler, bit her lip. "And *that's* a pretty cheap remark. You'd better go. Go, Mark, leave me alone. I don't want you here." She looked suddenly ill and half fell against a chair, pressing her hand to her eyes. He was instantly beside her, his face agonised.

"Caroline! Caroline – "

"Get me something," she said. "Mark, I feel awful. I'm – "

He got her some brandy quickly, and eased her into a chair. When she'd recovered he helped her to bed, where she lay watching him dully.

"Darling," he said presently, "if I sounded brutal I'm sorry. Try not to worry now. Just rest and recover."

"I'm sorry too," she murmured in a soft voice, almost a whisper. "I expect I'm difficult. But you see, I'm going to have a child, Mark. That's what makes it so much worse. Do you understand? *I'm going to have a child.*"

She started to sob, heavy exhausted crying which cut him to the heart. At the same time a great wave of relief swept over him. A child! That might explain it all. Women were frequently difficult at such times. All that she'd said – the way she'd acted – might only be due to her pregnancy. Her indifference to him too could be a symptom of her condition. Possibly when the baby was born things might be better between them. Clutching hard to the straw of hope, he softened.

"Darling, this will make a difference."

But she turned her head away.

"Oh, Mark, for goodness' sake don't be sloppy. I can't bear it. I don't want the child. Why should I?"

Why should she? He got up and walked to the window. No, why should she, since it was his child. Or was it? With the hope in him turning quickly, violently, to a renewed ugly suspicion, he strode back to the bedside.

"Caroline!"

"Yes?"

But when he looked at her lying there with the shadows dark under her eyes, he knew he could not ask the question. He turned away, his mind heavy with the thoughts which now, he knew, must torment him until he knew the truth, until he had found the courage to face his wife over this new and distressing possibility.

Chapter Sixteen

It was wet the next day, and as David Blair walked down the hill from the station, rain danced in blue puddles on the road. Looking round he decided that Port Todric in bad weather was really very much the same as other places. He half wished he hadn't come this time. The vacation was not very long, and he'd debated whether after all he wouldn't get more kick out of a week or two in Paris. But then, there was Caroline. She expected to see him; he'd promised, and he wanted to see her too. The affair hadn't yet cooled his ardour, although her last letter had been rather too urgent for his liking.

Darling,

You must come. It's important. Terribly, terribly important. I've got something to tell you, and I want to tell you quickly. So hurry, please hurry. There isn't much news. Mother still lectures me, and Mark is still obsessed by his school. The visitors are beginning to arrive here – a few new beards, both golden and black – but I am bored without you. The thrift will be out on the headlands when you get here. Do you remember that walk we had to Blind Man's Cove in July? How lovely it was with the flowers and sun, but the spring is best of all. I want to see the spring with you.

Write to me.

As ever,
Caroline.

Hmm, he had thought, on reading it. Altogether too emotional. She mustn't go falling in love with him – not in that way. He didn't want the responsibility of having to hurt her in the end. If he'd thought she was that kind of woman he'd have left her alone. But hang it all – she wasn't. Why, in the first five minutes of their being alone together she'd told him details of her life with her husband – emphasised certain difficulties – which no woman of scruples would do. She wasn't exactly blatant, of course. He couldn't *quite* make her out. Sometimes at unexpected moments she showed an odd naivety which could be discomfiting. All the same, she was no innocent. She 'knew the answers' all right, and this was 1927 – it was really absurd to have any conscience over her at all.

However, as he walked down the street to the hotel, Blair wasn't happy over the business. So long as she kept to the rules of the game, he could enjoy her with passion, as his mistress. But this urgency and sentiment was dangerous. He almost decided, on impulse, to go back to the station and take the first train to town. The next moment he was telling himself not to be a fool, and five minutes later was unpacking his bag in the hotel bedroom. From his window he had a good view of the harbour; the sea was grey now, the boats tossing on the water which flung its spume in great crests of foam against the rocks and sea wall.

Make a good sketch, he thought, and wondered whether to get out his pad forthwith. But a savoury smell of dinner from downstairs decided the question. He had a wash, changed his attire and presently went down for a meal.

He did not see Caroline that evening, but the following morning telephoned. Mark had already gone to the studio, so she was free to make arrangements without opposition. They decided to go to Praille in the afternoon, and Caroline told him she'd pick him up in the car outside the post office.

The rain had cleared, and by three o'clock the sun was shining brightly on the grey roofs of the town, giving a newly washed quality to the streets and windows. Beyond, the narrow road curled up ribbon-like to the moors above the sea. Gulls dipped and glided over the headlands, and a few clouds white and soft as wool floated above the hills on the left, where in the distance there rose the grim forbidding outline of Praille Quoit.

Not until they were well out of Port Todric was any personal discussion broached. Then Caroline stopped the car in a gap at the side of the road. He took her into his arms and found she was trembling. His senses responded as he'd half-hoped, half-feared they would. She was a sensuous creature – all subtle scent and curves.

"Caroline!"

"Oh, David – David!"

Her arms were round his neck, her lips clinging. He had meant to be more aloof with her this time, play for safety until he knew exactly where he stood. But propinquity weakened his armour, and after all why should he have qualms? She apparently had none.

A little later they drove on to Praille, where they had tea alone at a small cottage. The daylight was fading, and in the intimate warmth of firelight and shadows she told him – haltingly at first, more urgently as tension grew. He said nothing, did not even move. Meanwhile his mind was groping for realities. A child, she said – *his* child? But how did she know? And if so why hadn't she done something about it? It was fantastic, absurd. From the confusion of his own thoughts he switched his attention to what she was saying.

" – and I'm sure, David, I'm sure Mark would divorce me if we told him everything. You see, he knows I'm in love with you. And when he knows it's to be *your* baby . . ."

An abrupt movement of his head towards the door, a furtive, impatient, almost frightened movement, stopped her flow of words. She saw that he was angry.

"Why, David – "

"Don't be an idiot, Caroline," he said, "keep your voice down."

"Yes, but – you're not annoyed, are you? You love me, don't you? *Don't* you?"

He stared at her as though he'd not seen her before. "Of course I love you. As much as I can. But this other – well, it takes the wind out of my sails."

"You don't mean – it makes no difference, does it? Don't look at me like that. Does it? *Does* it?"

"Shh," he said. "Difference? Well, it's bound to, isn't it? I mean, a woman can't go having a baby and think it's going to make no difference."

"No, I suppose not, but – "

"You should have been more careful," he said. "Done something about it earlier. And, after all, how do you know it's *my* child?"

Her lips became set and unhappy. "I do know."

"Well," his voice was sulky, "it's more than I do."

She stared at him. "David, how can you! How *can* you!"

"Sorry," he mumbled. "But if it's true – I can't understand how you could have managed things so badly. These days too, when every woman knows how to avoid a kid if she doesn't want it."

"How do you know I don't want it?"

"Well, if you do, why get into such a state about it?"

"Do you mean – do you mean that you don't mind? That you – that you'll let Mark divorce me, and marry me then?"

"No, I don't," he spoke roughly, "so for heaven's sake, Caroline, get that out of your head."

She started to cry, and he gripped her arm hard. "Do *please* pull yourself together, or the whole place will hear." His urgent whisper was almost a hiss.

She dried her eyes and spoke in more normal tones. "Very well, I'll try. I'm sorry."

He sighed with relief, relaxed slightly, and softened. "Look here, darling," he said, "I don't want to hurt you, but honestly – this idea of divorce, it wouldn't do, don't you see? In the first place it could mess up my job. It isn't even as though I could *afford* to marry you. I don't even know that we'd be suited – not to be tied up together for life. I think a hell of a lot of you, darling, but it's not in me to care that way. I don't think you'd be happy either," he concluded miserably.

There was a pause in which is seemed to Caroline that the room reeled, darkened, then came into focus again. She could harly believe that David was saying these things to her. She had an impulse to jump up and rush away from him into the soothing cooling air, to run and run to some quiet place where she could be alone with her shock and unhappiness.

But after a brief interim she heard herself saying mechanically, "Perhaps not. I see, I understand."

Her acquiescence spurred him to a floundering rush of justification. "After all, more than likely it's Mark's child. I'm sorry to have given you all this worry, Caroline. I've been stupid, I guess, I can see it now. We both have. But you're so damned attractive, I suppose I just – "

"Don't!" Her eyes had a wild light in them. "Stop – I don't want to hear any more. It's *I've* been the fool to imagine that – to imagine – " She broke off, choking back her tears, then resumed. "But I did think you cared for me. The thought of being without you is so awful. I just don't – " she broke off in a rush of misery.

"There's no need to be without me," he told her, stroking her hand soothingly. "Darling, if you're sensible, what difference does it make? Try and face things as they are. *Please*."

But she appeared not to be listening. "I suppose," she went on, "after today you'll just go away and forget about me. That's it, that's what you want, isn't it?"

"No, it isn't," he answered angrily. "I'll be back for the holidays and we can be as we've always been when you've got this business over."

"In the summer?" she insisted.

"Yes, yes," he groaned. "Of course."

"Do you mean it? Or are you just saying things? If that's it you needn't I can assure you, you needn't."

"Of course I mean it," he promised her. He felt caught in a web of frustration and obligation, which for the moment changed his ardour to impatience. Sensing this she was silent, and their tea was concluded in an atmosphere of strain and tension which was unrelieved on their way back to Port Todric. With her gaiety gone she looked hard, almost old, sitting beside him with her lips set, her eyes miserable in her pale face.

The next day, however, she forced herself to a pitch of simulated lightheartedness which almost deceived him. Mark, aware that she was seeing David, tried to dull his suspicions and once more resorted to the unsatisfactory game of self-deception, telling himself that in two weeks Blair would be gone, after which he'd be free to get things straight with his wife.

At the end of the fortnight, however, he still shelved the issue. He knew Caroline was unhappy, he knew something had happened, but sensing her inner despair could not bring himself to inflict further pain upon her. Several times he tried, but always managed to evade the final confrontation.

Spring dragged by and summer came. In July David was to return. Mark waited for Caroline to make some mention of this. He would have welcomed a word, some tangible clue, which would have shown him where the land lay. But none came, and although he told himself he was being a fool, he still could not face upsetting her with questions or recriminations. He was afraid for her, and the child, and because of it did all he could to keep her fit and as content as possible. On the whole seemed happier with him than she'd been in recent months, but he felt sometimes, sadly, that it was the acquiescence of resignation rather than of any change of attitude towards himself.

Caroline expected her baby in October. She was entirely apathetic over it, concerned only for it to be over as soon as possible so that she might recover her figure, and incidentally David's interest. He'd written to her irregularly since his Easter visit. Luckily the post arrived when her husband had left for the studio. In his last note he'd told her that he'd soon appear and would probably be putting up at the Jolly Admiral. He'd get in touch with her when he arrived, about August the second or third. She mustn't worry, he wrote, and to buck up, 'everything would work out for the best'. What he meant by that she didn't know. All she could do was to wait day by day for the post.

Her nerves became gradually more torn by watching and waiting.

At last, a few days before she expected him, a letter arrived. It was a misty day, with a thin drizzle blown inland from the sea. The gulls came wheeling over the cliffs and the grey sky was filled with their mournful crying. Mark had gone to the studio, but the daily girl had not yet arrived. In her dressing gown, with her fair hair hanging in two plaits over her shoulders, Caroline ran to the door as soon as she heard the rattle of the box. The white envelope lay there with the familiar carefully typed address on it. For some moments she dare not open it, but stood tense and rigid staring at the postmark. Then, with trembling fingers, she tore it across. There was a pause in which the sheet of paper seemed to mock her, with it's cruel implication.

Dear Caroline,
I find after all that I shall not be able to make it this time. I've been frantically busy, and on top of everything have a fellow to coach through the break.

She stopped reading, then in a wave of hysteria, started to laugh. Of course not. She had known all the time really, all the time she had known. He had never meant to come. Presently she moved and went back to the sitting room. The cat, wanting its saucer of milk, came towards her, miaowing. She was still laughing. But after a minute or two her laughter changed to tears as the cat, arching, pressed against her legs.

"Oh, pussy!" she said, drawing the furry body to her. "Oh, pussy – what am I going to do now?"

If Mark sensed his wife's mood when he returned at midday, he did not comment on it, but when she went to fetch the car directly after lunch, he protested.

"But Caroline, you're never going out on a day like this? It's raining quite heavily. What's your idea?"

"I'm going for a run," she told him. "I'm tired of being cooped up. I've a headache."

"But – "

"Oh, Mark, *please*."

Seeing that she really was not well, hurt by the lonely, dazed look in her eyes, he said, "If you must, I'm coming with you."

"But the school?"

"Julia's looking in this afternoon, it'll be O.K. I'll call on the way back. You're not going out alone, Caroline, not as you are. Have you had a tablet or anything?"

She shook her head. "I shall be all right when I get out. Honestly. I'm *all right*."

"Oh, very well."

They took the road across the moors towards Beggar's Haven, a small hamlet lying between Penzance and Port Todric. As they climbed the steep winding hill the rain changed to mist again blowing across the gorse and heather in filmy curling shapes visible one moment, gone the next, like ghosts waving their thin arms in the air. Occasionally there appeared for a second the distorted pale gleam of some cottage or ruin, emerging skeleton-like through the greyness. Up and up they climbed, as though into the sky itself, while clouds of drizzle swept against the windscreen, penetrating into the car, where it clung in glistening drops to Caroline's hair. Everything appeared pale and meaningless to her, an empty chill holding only a sense of dull futility.

The car turned abruptly round the corner into Beggar's Haven, passed the small group of cottages, and started down the steep incline to the bottom road. Below, curling voids of vapour lay waiting to receive them. Her mood changed to slowly mounting exhilaration. She turned glittering eyes on Mark.

"Let me drive," she said.

"When we get to the bottom," he answered.

The main road at the foot of the hill led straight and smooth along the coast back to Port Todric. Its surface glimmered white in the drizzle, bordered on either side by the vague shape of hedges looming grotesquely, and to the right the uncertain haze of the sea.

Some way before the crossroads Caroline took the wheel. She drove slowly at first, responding to the thrum of the engine and feel of the wheel under her hands. Gradually, the strange sense of mounting excitement grew. Pressure on the accelerator increased. The dim shapes became wilder, the blown clouds of mist falling away like defeated angels as the car streamed along. She had a sudden swift feeling that this was escape and victory. Victory over her own life and its despair; escape from David's betrayal. As she sped on it seemed to her that all the lesser parts of her existence, the small petty trivialities, led up to this one gesture, this superb blind drive towards self-extinction.

She became aware at one moment of Mark's voice shouting

in her ear, "Carol, for God's sake!" Felt his hand on the wheel, clutching it. She increased the pressure on the accelerator. The car lurched forward again, steadied and gathered speed while the speedometer mounted up and up – and the world raced to meet them. Then, like two stars, lights loomed ahead through the fog. Mark flung himself over her body towards the brake, but it was too late. When, in a flash of reason, she would have diverted the course, the bus was already upon them; there was the deafening sound of splintering glass and torn metal, the impact of gears and a human shriek. Then darkness.

When their bodies were recovered from the debris, Mark was found to have been killed outright. By some miracle Caroline, though badly injured about the head, was still alive. She was taken to hospital, and lived long enough to give birth prematurely to twins, a boy and a girl.

She died the same night with Julia beside her. Her eyes, when she opened them, had the same old clear pristine quality of childhood. She smiled and tried to speak.

"Mother, I – " but that was as far as she got. A moment later her eyes closed and she did not regain consciousness. From the cot not far away there came the primitive thin wailing of the newly born.

Chapter Seventeen

When the babies were strong enough to leave hospital Julia had them brought to her own home. Although she did not entirely relish the thought of having the sole care of two young things she felt she could do no less, neither did she wish to. For in a sense they were hers, more in one way than they had ever been Caroline's, who had not wanted them or lived to notice them.

From their earliest infancy Julia could see not the slightest resemblance to their mother. These children were darker, and after the first few months, sturdier. They cried lustily, and had none of the frail fairy-like qualities that had been Caroline's as a small child. The knowledge was relief to Julia. She had never understood her daughter. Caroline indeed had been a misfit into an age which had destroyed her. These children were different. They should not be spoiled as Caroline had been spoiled. She would teach them to have their feet on the earth.

She need have no fears on this score. For from first learning to toddle the twins were as jolly and naughty a pair of babies as any to be found. She called them Stephen and Sarah. Stephen after her husband, and Sarah in memory of her own mother. When they were a year old she had their surname altered to Kerr; this was, she thought, a simpler and possibly more honest state of affairs since, from the very beginning, she had doubted that they were Mark's children. The knowledge, curiously, did not worry her very much. They were her own – of her blood. Sarah, though darker, was not unlike old photographs of herself as a child, and Stephen bore a certain resemblance to his grandfather. The smile was the same, the unruly curly hair and laughing eyes. But he was solid and direct; there was no subtlety about Stephen. He had all Richard Benson's attack and stubbornness. What he wanted he went for and screamed when he could not get it. Sarah too had a temper, but it was more imperious, demanding. She had a quicker imagination than Stephen, and showed as a child a distinct capacity for drawing.

When they were three years old, Julia had to get rid of the extra help she'd had in the house, owing to a further decrease in her father's money. A great many of Richard Benson's securities had been in shares which after the war had steadily declined. Now, in her middle forties, she once more found herself having to face an expenditure which, without careful planning, would easily exceed her income. What remained of the capital of course would be the children's when they grew up. But Julia no longer trusted the future. No one knew what might lie ahead, and she wished to keep sufficient in hand to send the twins to good schools when they were a little older. The running of the studio also cost her more than in previous years. Since Mark's death she had had to employ someone to run it – a man with academic credentials, Roger Weir, whose salary swallowed up a large percentage of the profits. But he was a man of imagination, with ideas in line with Stephen's and Mark's, and so long as she drew a certain amount she did not mind. Her own work meanwhile was seriously curtailed. At nights when the twins had gone to bed she forced her tired body and flagging imagination to working pitch. But the output was not of her best, and in the end she deferred her serious writing in favour of an easier and more lucrative means of income – a weekly article in a women's magazine, which she obtained through her reputation as a novelist.

When they were five years old, Sarah and Stephen were sent to Port Todric council school. Julia had none of her father's snobbery about education. Caroline was an example of what an expensive education had or had not done. When they were twelve or so the twins should go to a decent school of her choice; meanwhile it would not hurt them to rough it a little and mix with every type of youngster.

Certainly they seemed to get on all right, although Stephen

took every chance of avoiding school when he could. Once, when he was seven years old, he disappeared for a whole day, returning at eight o'clock at night with a half-apologetic, half-tentative grin on his rosy face, telling Julia calmly that he had been out in old Peter Perryn's boat. Julia, who had been half frantic when he did not return after school, even getting into touch with the police, had rushed down to old Peter who had no idea, apparently, that the boy had not been given permission, since he had concocted some tale that had satisfied him. Julia, in the first reaction of relief and anger, felt temporarily defeated and unable to deal with her unruly grandson. Physical punishment was abhorrent to her. Yet what was the answer? How would Stephen have dealt with the situation? Shaking, she sat down. Seeing her distress, the little boy was immediately at her knees, staring up at her.

"What's the matter, Nan? I'm all right. Don't look like that."

"Oh, Stephen," she said, "don't you realise that I love you, and that when you go off like that I get all sorts of terrible ideas? Anything might have happened. It was cruel of you."

He looked puzzled for a moment, then blurted out, "I'm sorry. But there wasn't any need to worry. Old Peter runs a boat fine. We caught lots of fish."

Julia sighed. "We're not talking about fish," she pointed out. "You told him a fib as well as giving me the fright of my life. And that's wrong. Understand?"

"I s'pose. But I didn't really fib. I just let him *think* things. And I was seeing what it was like, having a boat, 'cos when I grow up *I* want one and to be like old Peter and go fishing at nights."

"Well, there's time to decide that later," Julia said. "Maybe you will if you're a good boy."

"Guess I'm not the good kind," Stephen said solemnly. "The good boys at school are awful dull. You've no idea."

"Well," Julia said, "I expect *you* to be good, anyhow."

"Sarah isn't always," he insisted. "You should just see *her* at school sometimes – bloody awful."

"Don't use that word, Stephen! I won't have it."

"Well, Cocky does."

"And who's Cocky?"

116

"He's our football captain. He's a jolly fine chap."

"That may be, but you needn't copy his language," Julia said, realising the next moment she must sound rather prim. Youngsters really were so hard to get through to in their own language.

Sarah was more secretive and silent than her brother, and a good deal cleverer; consequently she was not nearly so often in trouble. But Julia did not differentiate; she treated both with equal understanding and occasional severity when they deserved it. The method seemed to pay. On the whole they were loving and comparatively amenable. Julia was attached to them as she had never been to Caroline. There was, she decided, a good deal too much talk of psychology nowadays. Children did not so much want psychology as affection, and the knowledge there were some things in life that must be respected and obeyed.

Sometimes on a Saturday afternoon or Sunday they all went off together to Blind Man's Cove, where they picnicked and bathed afterwards. They grew brown and healthy as gipsies, and Julia at these times felt almost young herself. She was a little stouter than she used to be, but her hair was luxurious and abundant still, and she was as nimble and quick on her feet as a girl. After bathing they would race along the sands together to get warm; then, panting and full of joy and fresh air, climb the steep path back up the cliff. Sometimes, when she was tired, she would tell the children to bathe, while she herself would lie on the sand with sewing or a book. But always for her, the cove was a happy place, filled with the beauty of light and shade, the water lovely as only Cornish waters could be – shot with translucent colours of every tone – jade, amber, deep seagreen, and palest, purest mauve and lemon. She would think at these times how lucky she had been in her life. There had been shadows and dark patches, as there were in the waves lapping at her feet. But through it had run always the thread and undercurrent of beauty, something of which continued, carried on the strong tide of her love which had begun so many years ago with Stephen, her husband.

Once Sarah, coming upon her sitting there lost in her reflections, said, "What are you thinking of Nan?"

117

"Oh, just thoughts, darling. You wouldn't understand. I was thinking that life was rather like a pattern, that's all."

"But I do understand," Sarah said solemnly – she was just eight years old – "of course I do. I've thought of it myself – how you can make it do what you like, like this." She took some wet sand in her hands and moulded it into the shape of a ball.

Julia laughed.

"Well, not quite so easily as that perhaps," she said. "You can't do *everything* you want, you know, Sarah, but you can make the most of what you're given." Then, thinking she must sound "preachified", she added with another laugh, "Anyhow, what a solemn subject for such a lovely afternoon."

"I like solemn subjects," Sarah said, "so long as they're not lessons. I mean, I like thinking things out for myself. I like *making* things. You know, Nan – "

"What sort of things?" queried Julia.

"Things you can see and hold," Sarah went on, her eyes shining. "We can do modelling at school now. I like that. Sometimes you can make just what you like, and then it's put in an oven and cooked."

"Oh?" Julia was interested. "You haven't shown me any."

"No, I'm keeping them until I've done something really good," Sarah went on, "then I will."

Though she was so good at creative work, Sarah hid her efforts as long as she could rather than displaying them. Stephen on the other hand boasted about his, which were correspondingly and amusingly bad.

One afternoon, when they were ten years old, Julia, as a birthday treat, took the children to the circus in Penzance. Afterwards they went back to Port Todric and had tea at a cafe there, where there were special ices.

They were ready to leave, Julia had already paid the bill, and was putting the change into her purse, when a man came through the door. He started slightly as their eyes met, hesitated, then came forward. The face was familiar to her but at first she couldn't place him. There was a brief pause before memory suddenly registered. Of course! David Blair. Her face hardened. Had it been possible she would have passed him without speaking – and have avoided a ridiculous and unpleasant situation. But he gave her no opportunity. With his hand extended he remarked, "Mrs Kerr, isn't it?"

"It is, yes. And you, of course, are Mr Blair."

"Quite right. Nice to see you. It's a long time since I was down here – ten years or more."

"Just a little more, I think," Julia said with undue sweetness.

His smile faded. She saw that he was staring at the children. She saw more – something that gave her a quick instinctive sensation of fear, and in that brief moment proof beyond all question that she had been right about him and Caroline. The knowledge that flashed between them was mutual. Her hand tightened on Sarah's shoulder instinctively.

"Well, Mr Blair, we are in rather a hurry. I have had my two granchildren out for tea. It is their birthday, you know, and so if you'll excuse me?"

He smiled ironically, almost impudently, but beyond his irony she sensed that he was touched, perturbed – moved against his will.

"Of course," he said, "but won't you – I mean, we shall meet again, I hope?" his eyes had gone back to Sarah.

"Oh, maybe," Julia said lightly, "but it's rather unlikely. The children are at school and I'm a busy woman. We don't go out much."

She gave him no more opportunity to question or play for time, but managed with admirable dexterity to extricate herself and the children from further complications.

When they were outside again Sarah said, "Nan, who was that man?"

"Oh, someone I used to know a long time ago."

"I didn't like him," Sarah said. "Not much."

"He had funny eyes," Stephen went on. "Like yours, Sarah. Yes, just like yours."

"Oh, come along, Stephen," Julia said impatiently, "or we shall never get home tonight."

"But they *were*," he persisted, "they were green like hers, Nan, and they had dark bits in them and a yellow line round."

"You notice things that aren't there, young man," Julia said, discomfited by his observation.

"Anyhow, they *were* like Sarah's eyes."

"They weren't."

"They were."

"Oh, children, stop quarrelling at once and come along," Julia cried, "or I shan't take you anywhere again."

She was annoyed, but knew quite well that Stephen was right. The eyes of Sarah were also the eyes of David Blair. She must be thankful that at the moment that was as far as the resemblance went – that, and a certain arrogant way of holding the head. Butt what did it matter? The children were hers, and Blair only a shadow temporarily resurrected. In a short time he would doubtless be gone again. In any case, he could do nothing, nothing at all. She had nothing to fear, they could not be taken from her now.

Chapter Eighteen

When she was twelve Sarah went to a Grammar School in Penzance, and Stephen to the corresponding boys' school there. Sarah was happy, but Stephen liked it no less and no better than the school at Port Todric. On the whole, perhaps, he had preferred the latter, since he was used to it, and in the daytime was nearer to his favourite haunts and fishermen cronies. By that time he could manage a small boat as well as any man, and Julia began to see that whatever he did in the future, it would obviously be something to do with the sea and boats. He was not, and never would be, the scholarly type, and had no taste for learning in any shape. But the sea was his friend and love. From his grandfather, Stephen's father, the Cornish fisherman, he must have inherited his passion for it; he even had the seaman's eyes – clear brilliant blue which always seemed to look a little beyond the immediate horizon into the far distance. With his curly hair, straight figure, and his happy smile in his bronzed face, Stephen was indeed good to look upon, and the more so when he returned to the shore from some jaunt or other, rime clinging to his face and hair, laughing, with his teeth glinting white in the sun.

Julia loved him. She loved him with a passion she never felt for Sarah. But it was Sarah who held her interest – Sarah, she knew, who some day must carry the reins, who might in the future forge another link in the heritage founded by herself and Stephen. Because of the girl's intelligence and the fact she had a mind to be reckoned with, Julia could regard her more logically and clearly, a little less personally. Stephen was all heart and feelings, but Sarah had direction and

121

motive. She also had force. She had already made up her mind to be a sculptor.

"It won't stop me helping at the studio," she said to Julia one day. "I could go to the Art School in Penzance first, couldn't I, Nan? Then I could start a sculpture class for you."

"We'll see," Julia said. She would not give any promise. Sarah had distinct ability, and might merit training. But it would depend on what they could afford.

The twins had been going to Penzance to school for six months when war broke out. Julia was fifty-six, and still, despite household duties, took certain responsibilities in the studio. Now she insisted upon volunteering for first aid services. At first, buoyed up by the excitement, the tension of knowing that the nation had its back to the wall and that she was one of that vast unit, she did not unduly feel the strain, but as the months passed it began to tell upon her insidiously. She went to bed at nights too tired to sleep for a long time, lying tense and ill-at-ease, feeling quite unable to cope effectively with the next day's events. Nevertheless, she managed, and by 1942 had steeled herself to a rhythm of life which included nervous strain as but a part of her day-to-day programme. A year later, Roger Weir left the studio to join the Air Force, and Julia once more began the chore of finding a replacement. She advertised, but had no suitable replies. The war was taking indiscriminate toll of all available men, and it appeared unlikely at that juncture that she would find the person she wanted. She interviewed two women, both too old and unimaginative to fulfil the needs of the group, and in despair started going down there each day herself.

There were now only ten regular students, seven youngsters, and three elderly men. The latter were content to dabble about on their own, but the younger needed attention. Well, then, there was nothing to do but tackle it herself. And so she took out all Stephen's old sketches, read up his notes, and immersed herself in a thorough study of the Stephen Kerr technique. The result was not so bad as might have been feared, although she had a guilty sense sometimes of being but a substitute for the real thing which, when she was tired, depressed her. Would Stephen have wanted her to go on like this? she thought one evening when she was clearing up after the students had gone. Or should she sell?

For some reason she felt excessively tired that night. She supposed it was the extra war work on top of the problems of housekeeping. For a moment or two, after putting the drawing boards away, she paused by the window with her hands on the sill. The pale evening light fell slantwise across the room throwing queer long shadows over the floors and walls – shadows that moved slightly as the draught blew the curtains. And in that brief interim time seemed to slip back. A momentary dizziness swept over her, then cleared, leaving her with the strange sensation of being a girl again. She was once more with Stephen seeing the studio as it had been thirty-five years ago. The empty room was peopled from the past, the very air seemed vibrant with memories of Stephen's laugh and voice. She quivered as the wind touched her shoulder, for surely that was her husband's touch upon her?

"Stephen," she whispered, and waited. And very slowly the conviction grew upon her that he was there beside her. She had only to move a step forward and his arms would be round her.

She knew then that she could not yet renounce the fruit of his energies and ambitions. Whatever lay ahead for the Stephen Kerr school, the responsibility for it was hers for as long as she could carry on.

Minutes later she moved, and automatically fastened the lockers before leaving for the night. As she stepped outside into the cool evening, the wail of a siren sounded dismally across the harbour. In the distance she heard the sinister drone of planes above the crying of the gulls. She remembered that she was on duty at the First Aid Post, and quickened her steps down the street. Few people were about now; the stars were bright in the sky above the sea. Beauty and menace so inextricably mixed! She shivered as she hurried along. This was the world that Sarah and young Stephen had come into. What lay in the future? What would they be able to make of it? Would they be strong enough to create decency and balance for themselves from the disorder of civilization? For it was only the strong who could survive; the old laws of nature still held good. The weak were

123

destroyed or destroyed themselves as Caroline had done. But Sarah and Stephen, they were all right – good stuff. There was something in them both that had the enduring quality of the hills and the very rocks, something that would stand strong as Praille Quoit stood on its towering moor.

"Everything's going to be all right, Stephen," she whispered as she walked along, "everything's going to be all right."

And she felt he heard and understood – was satisfied. There was comfort in this contact beyond death which strengthened her. She had never been orthodox, but she knew that life had a pattern which one day must be made clear – a pattern of beauty and tragedy mixed, which one must taste to the full before the meaning was revealed. That one had to suffer and grow old was but a drawing out of the thread to its appointed conclusion. But other threads went on and on into the future, so that really one's link was never cut.

The air seemed alive with the battling of great unseen wings now, which had put the birds to flight. A dog barked shrilly from a cottage nearby. The next moment the battering of distant anti-aircraft began.

Stephen and Sarah would be home from school. She was glad of that. Mrs Trewella from next door would have asked them in, as she always did when there was a raid. This left Julia free to tackle her duties at the post without undue anxiety over the children.

Hours later she returned to the house. All was quiet; not even a breath of wind to disturb the peace. There was a faint scent of flowers in the dusk. Before inserting her key into the door, she drew a deep breath, then with her hand on the latch she went in.

Home, she thought with relief. Why did there have to be wars and disagreements? Why hadn't human beings yet learned to live in harmony?

Only God knew the answer. And God, sometimes, seemed very far away.

Chapter Nineteen

Somehow Julia managed to keep the studio going until the end of the war. In the last year of it, 1945, Stephen joined the Merchant Service, and a few months later sailed from Plymouth for a destination unknown to her. The house seemed unbearably quiet without him. Both she and Sarah tried to hide their fears from each other, but in both it was there – the painful thought of young Stephen in danger, under fire.

"Still," Julia said once, speaking her thoughts aloud, "it's what he wanted. He always loved the sea. And most likely he'll come through all right. And it's great work – if it wasn't for our food ships we should be nowhere."

"Of course," Sarah agreed. "And somehow I don't think anything'll happen to Stephen. It *couldn't*. He's too alive. Don't worry, Nan, I'm sure it'll be all right."

Julia then could not help comparing the girl's admirable self-control with the abandoned hysteria of Caroline, her mother, when her own father had joined up in the first war.

Sarah was still drawing and modelling hard; she also helped Julia with her various war duties. But following Stephen's departure, an inner restlessness seized her.

"Perhaps *I* ought to do something?" she said to Julia one day. "A proper job, I mean, a war job."

"But, Sarah, it's only a month or two since you left school," Julia said. "You're only seventeen. Wait a little."

"I'd thought of the Land Army," Sarah went on, "there are some girls in it younger than me, and I think I'd like growing things."

"But your hands," Julia said, "they'd get into a mess, and if

125

you want to go on with your art and sculpting later– "

"I don't think it would hurt *that*," Sarah said thoughtfully. "You know, Nan, there's a kind of relationship somewhere between soil and making things."

"What do you mean, dear?"

"I'm not quite sure," Sarah went on, "because I've never tried it, but I think I should like the feel of the earth. I think it would be such experience – such a *real* experience."

"You're looking at it romantically, I'm afraid," Julia said. "It's very hard work, and you're not used to physical labour of that kind."

Nevertheless, Sarah had her way. Soon after this conversation with her grandmother she joined the W.L.A. and Julia had to admit to herself that never had the child looked prettier or happier than when she set off in her breeches and green jersey for her first job on a moorland farm ten miles or so from Port Todric.

Contrary to all Julia's predictions, she liked the work, and most weeks, when she managed to come over by bus to see Julia, was full of her experiences, of hoeing and planting, and her amusing tussles with an obstinate pig called Billy. She also spoke a good deal of a young man called Peter Storm, the son of a neighbouring farmer who bred prize cattle.

"You should just see his place, Nan," she said once. "It's like a manor house, really, with a drive up to it, and meadows on each side filled with buttercups, and the back of the house slopes to the sea through pine woods."

"Oh," said Julia. "What's it called?"

"Poldragon," Sarah answered. "It's very old. It's belonged to the family for ages. *I* should be awfully proud to have a home like that, but Peter isn't – I mean, not in a conceited way. You know, Nan, he's very democratic and all that."

"How did you meet him?" asked Julia.

"Oh, well, everyone knows everyone in such a small place, and we had to go over to fetch some fertilizer stuff once. But I've met him at the dances, too."

"The village dances?"

Sarah nodded. "They're awful fun. Everyone mixes – villagers and people like Sir John Borlaze the squire. And – oh, I dunno – life's so interesting, Nan. I wouldn't have missed this for anything."

"Good," said Julia, trying to stifle faint misgivings over the young man. "But don't go falling in love yet, Sarah, you've got lots to do before that."

Sarah laughed. "Don't be silly. Falling in *love*! Why should I? Still, he's terribly nice, as a friend, I mean, and to dance with and talk to sometimes."

Julia let the subject drop. But as the weeks went by she became aware of a deepening seriousness in the girl, a thoughtfulness which could not entirely be put down to her interest in the growing of crops.

Peace came, and Julia's fears for Stephen were at an end. He returned for a short time afterwards, informing her that he would be in the service probably for another year, perhaps two.

"Then," he said with a grin, "back home to my boat."

"Your boat?" queried Julia, "what do you mean, Stephen?"

He paused before replying. "Would you mind awfully, Nan, if I just turned into a simple sort of fellow like Curnow and old Tom Polglase and had my own fishing boat?"

"A fisherman?" Julia laughed. "Still clinging to your childhood dream? It seems so odd somehow. It won't be long before you have a little money of your own. Not much, but enough to let you have a training of some sort, and to give you a certain security. Are you sure?"

"Yes, I *am* sure," Stephen said with sudden enthusiasm. "I've always been sure. I'm not clever, I never have been. But I love the sea, Nan, I could make a go of that."

"A '*go*'?"

"I mean, I'd be happy," he told her. "And after all, isn't that what counts? Gosh! To think of being back at Port Todric and going out with the other fellows at nights! The Service isn't bad, but this would be different – I'd be my own master, Nan, think of it!"

Yes, she thought to herself watching him, he was cut out for it. His heart's in it.

They did not discuss the matter further at that point. But Julia knew that Stephen had his mind made up. She supposed

127

everything considered he might do many worse things. As he said, he wasn't clever. To think of him tied to an office stool was out of the question. He belonged to the out-of-doors. But Sarah was a different problem. Julia hoped sincerely she wouldn't want to grow carrots and potatoes for the rest of her life.

She didn't.

Sarah arrived home one day in the autumn of 1945 saying she had left the farm, and meant now to help Julia with the school.

"But, darling – " Julia said, surprised. "This is all so sudden. The last time you were here you didn't say a word about it. What's happened to make you change your mind?"

Sarah did not look entirely happy.

"Oh, I dunno – things," she said slowly. "You see Peter thought – "

"Ah! Peter."

"Yes." Sarah lips closed tightly. Julia waited, until of her own accord she continued, "Well, Nan, as a matter of fact – Peter and I – you see – "

"Yes?"

"We *do* rather like each other," Sarah admitted, "only – "

"You mean you think you're in love with each other?"

"We *are*," Sarah stated definitely. "We have been for ages, I think."

"But, Sarah, you don't know your own mind yet."

"Oh, yes, I do," Sarah said with sudden decision. "Too much. That's just it."

"Sarah, do explain what you mean."

"Well," she said, with an impetuous toss of her head, "Peter thinks we should be married immediately, but – "

"At eighteen? Ridiculous."

"It isn't that," Sarah said quickly. "Age has nothing to to do with it. I shan't change my mind or anything like that, Nan, and I'd simply love to live at Poldragon. Only, well – "

"Yes?"

"You see, there's another side of me that Peter doesn't know, that he wouldn't believe in, even if he did. I'm talking of my work – my *real* work. So you see first of all I've got to *prove* it to him."

"I see." Julia's voice was sympathetic. "You mean your modelling and carving?"

Sarah nodded. "That's half of me, Nan. I couldn't just get married and stifle it, could I?"

"Of course not," Julia agreed warmly.

"And so I thought I'd work at the studio *first*, until I made some sort of a reputation – because I *can*, I know I can – and then perhaps, when Peter saw, he'd understand."

"Tell me, darling," Julia asked, "is he the sort of young man who'd expect you to have no interests of your own? Because if he is, Sarah, and you ever *do* marry him – marriage, you know, must be the full-time job. No two people can live happily divided against each other. Both the man and the woman – if they are to make a success of it – must either put the other first, or determine at the beginning to be generous to each other. I had to learn this in my life with your grandfather. And it wasn't easy."

"But Peter isn't like that – he *wouldn't* be if he really thought I could do anything," Sarah persisted. "That's just why I've got to *show* him. So that we can start square."

"I see what you mean," Julia agreed, a little touched and amused by Sarah's phraseology. 'Start square'. She was grateful for the girl's confidence in her. Indeed there was nothing at all deceitful in Sarah. Strong-willed she might be. Nothing would alter her opinion if she really considered herself to be in the right. But she was frank always about her actions, and if questioned would never resort to a lie. And Julia wondered afresh that Caroline should have bred children so utterly unlike her in character.

She recollected, with pain, that there had been a time when Caroline herself had professed interest in the studio, but that had been bogus and short-lived. Indeed, Caroline's tragedy had been that she had never found herself sufficiently to be true to one thing or one person. With Sarah it was different. Julia realised that when the child suggested helping with the group she really meant it, and nothing just then would have given her greater pleasure than to have had help with her problems there. She now had an assistant – an artist who had been wounded at the end of the war, but owing to nervous strain and shock was not proving entirely satisfactory. He was dictatorial in method, and already making enemies with the local Art Society with whom Julia had managed to keep on good terms until then.

Someone like Sarah, therefore, would have been a support, but of course she was as yet too untrained and young. And in any case, with her talent she should be given greater chances if she were really serious in her intention to carry on with her sculpting.

However, it was not until the spring of 1946 that Sarah was prevailed upon by Julia to go to London to an art college for training. Peter, frankly upset, had not understood at all.

On the evening before she went, he came over to Port Todric where Julia welcomed him warmly, because from the little she had seen of him she liked the young man, and because Sarah had not acted foolishly and allowed him to stand in her way.

But in the evening, when he went with Sarah for a walk along the cliffs, he made one more effort to dissuade her from what seemed to him a needless separation.

"It's just silly," he pointed out. "You say you love me, and yet you take the first chance to go romping off after a career."

Sarah sighed, and took his arm. He was such a dear, and yet really so childish despite his twenty-six years.

"Oh, Peter, but we've talked all that out," she said. "Don't spoil things by arguing about it again."

"We've never talked it out, you mean *you* have. I've never had any say in it at all. You've just done exactly what you want, Sarah, from the very beginning."

Her jaw set obstinately. "Well, I've not misled you. If you wanted to marry some little-stay-at-home, Peter, you shouldn't have chosen me."

"There you go again. The first objection I make and you go threatening to throw me over."

"No, I *didn't*," she said indignantly. "You're twisting my words. Anyhow, I'm not ready to be married yet."

"Thanks a lot."

"If I married you now without ever proving what I could do—"

"Oh, darling, you sound just like a book."

"Well, it's true. I know you don't believe me, but it *is* true.

130

It's something *inside* of me, Peter, I've got to get it out somehow. I've always *meant* to, and if I never had a shot, well I'd just – I'd just feel kind of thwarted about it all my life. And you never know," she added sagaciously, "I might turn into a nagger, Peter. You wouldn't like that."

He couldn't help laughing. "It seems cock-eyed to me, anyhow."

"And then there's Nan. I owe it to her," Sarah went on. "She's had such a lot of disappointments, you know, losing grandfather, and then mother and everything – "

"Oh, that's an excuse," he retorted. "You want to go for *yourself*, Sarah, make no mistake about it."

"Yes, I do," she flashed. "And if you weren't so old-fashioned, you'd understand."

"Well, I'm afraid I don't."

They walked on in silence, where the twilight deepened over the headland and the rocks changed to blue against the paler glitter of the sea. Across the water the dark shapes of fishing boats were putting out for the night, and over the water came the mournful crying of gulls.

Suddenly Sarah turned impulsively to him, her eyes bright. "Peter," she said urgently, "I do love you. You know that, don't you? Oh, Peter, nothing matters in comparison. It's because of that, partly, that I'm going. It won't be long, and you'll come and see me, won't you? Just imagine it – meeting you in London, knowing that we're going to be married. We can make plans, and we can talk about everything – "

"Yes," he agreed, "provided you don't change your mind."

"Change my mind!" she cried with a laugh that was half a sob. "Don't be bats, Peter. Oh, don't be a fool, kiss me."

He did so, gently at first, then more passionately, knowing he could no longer fight her, she had won. Half of him was not sorry. It showed that she had a mind of her own, was worth winning. But he was far from understanding her. And he very much doubted if he ever would completely. Still, women were mysterious creatures, and Sarah obviously was no exception to the rule. So long as she loved him he'd put up with it.

Presently, hand in hand, they walked on again, while the sky darkened and soon the first star appeared over the sea. All was very quiet.

"I shall remember this evening all my life," Sarah said, "even when I'm old – you and me, and this stillness. Don't you feel a sort of promise in the air? I do. I'm sure we're going to have a wonderful life together, Peter."

"So am I. I'll see to that."

She smiled in the darkness – a subtle, confident little smile. Dear Peter! She would make him proud of her, so that later, when they were married, he would realise that she had been right to go away.

Chapter Twenty

Following Sarah's departure. Julia was confronted with the question of economy once more. This was essential now. Her last book had not been a particularly good seller despite favourable press reviews; consequently her royalties were small, and she had, as well, to face the additional expense of Sarah's art college training, which seriously cut into the income from her father's money. The school was doing quite well, but Richard Kent, the new assistant, had a considerably larger salary than any of his predecessors, and was as well favouring a certain group of painters that had suddenly sprung into prominence since the war. Julia considered this was not good for the Kerr Group. She was not, she hoped, unduly bigotted, but a shrewd streak in her believed that many who came to Port Todric now were escapists taking cover under a form of decadence or self-delusion which was but the outcome of the war. Her blood boiled at the thought of Stephen's school getting into the hands of a pseudo-group espousing risky morals, scrounging habits, and a mode of life that was entirely repellent to her. In honest objective moments she admitted to herself she might be prejudiced; perhaps she was getting narrow-minded in her old age. She tried to be fair, but however diligent her attempts she could not reconcile the idea of 'genius' with young men who borrowed money, got drunk on it the same night, and the next day had the effrontery to exhibit paintings of one-sided women with one eye on the forehead and one eye on the breast, priced at a hundred guineas. In some ways she was fundamentally too conservative to realise any merit in the new ideas and new ideology in art and living which was to shape the future.

"I don't want this kind of work associated with the Stephen Kerr School," she said sharply one day to Kent. "My husband had very definite ideas on some matters which should, I think, be followed as closely as possible."

Kent's pannish eyebrows arched themselves perceptibly higher as he said drily, "But your husband died thirty years ago, Mrs Kerr."

"Just what do you mean?" asked Julia, though she knew very well.

He shrugged. "Well, styles change. There are periods in art. It would be stupid to try and retain a worn out technique – "

"Stephen's work and ideas were not like that," Julia retorted quickly. "The best art does not date. Surely that's the test of it. And I'm not so old-fashioned that I'd want to rule out modern movements. Some present-day work is good, and when it's good it's exciting. I don't care a fiddle-dee-dee whether it's traditional, impressionistic, abstract or whatever you like to call it, so long as it's got merit. But we mustn't allow pseudo stuff in *our* school, Mr Kent."

Afterwards she became aware that she might have sounded slightly bigotted. But really! If she let Kent have his way entirely he'd fill the studio with long-haired, bearded young men who hadn't the least idea what they were even *trying* to express with their blots and smudges and twisted torsos. And apart from the aesthetic point of view, there were the practical issues to consider. She simply could not afford at the moment to let the school lose any kudos or prospective members. Indeed, her pressing problem was how to cut expenses.

With this in mind she decided abruptly one day that her best course was to move into a smaller house. With the children grown up and away it seemed senseless to continue where she was when she could live far cheaper elsewhere. And so she began to look about for a suitable place. Strangely enough both fate and sentiment played into her hands. Mrs Tremayne had died the previous year, and the house had afterwards been converted into more modern flats which were shortly to be let. The ground floor had been snapped up, but the house agent, who knew Julia well, told her that 7a was not yet let, and if she liked she could have the first refusal. Julia, of course, agreed to look over it that same day. A momentary pang made her pause on the step before entering the door that same afternoon. How odd it was again to be on the threshold of the rooms where, almost forty years ago, she and Stephen had first bearded Mrs T, and started their married life together. A host of familiar scenes swept through her brain as she went in – their first night together, Mrs Tremayne's cross-examination, the numerous little misunderstandings and reconciliations, the daily small happenings, her flight later to Trelissey and her return with Stephen. Comedy and tragedy, humour, tears! How vital it had been, how important everything had seemed then. And now here she was, an ageing woman, despite her erect figure and youthful face, about to come back. For she knew she *would* come back. In a sense it was a natural return.

The flat, of course, had been altered almost beyond recognition, with a proper water system installed and electric light. The walls were distempered in a gay primrose yellow throughout; another room had been added as well. It was really very charming.

If only Stephen could see it, Julia thought as she made arrangements forthwith to take the place. When she remembered the awful sofa he'd covered with her shawl and the way he stuck his pictures on the damp patches, she smiled.

And yet it had been exciting. Would it after all have been quite as much fun to come into it as it was now, so modern and clean and newly painted?

A month later she was installed again in 7a. The satisfaction of knowing she was now more likely to keep comfortably within her means inspired her with a burst of fresh energy. She went down more frequently to the studio, and what she saw there strengthened her growing conviction that sooner or later she must come to open conflict with Kent. The confrontation however was brought about unexpectedly through a source she had not contemplated – the Cornish Painters' Guild.

She had just finished her meal one evening and was clearing

the table, when there was a rap on the door. She was surprised to see Richard Ainsworth, the Chairman of the Committee, standing there impeccably clad as usual, in his carefully pressed grey suit and bow tie, his small imperial beard giving him a Frenchified appearance. He apologised for the lateness of his call, and when Julia asked him in was careful, before coming to the point of his visit, to praise her room and surroundings, and to comment upon her appearance. But Ainsworth was like that – Julia knew him – diplomatic in his flattery, his brain meanwhile darting shrewdly hither and thither behind his quick bird-like eyes. She guessed that what he had to say was not entirely pleasant. His thin elegant hands were moving restlessly at his sides. He was not entirely at ease.

"Well," said Julia presently, "and what is it you want of me, Mr Ainsworth?"

"Want of you, my dear lady?" Ainsworth said. "I can assure you you're quite wrong. My visit, to the contrary, is on your behalf."

"Indeed?"

"You have, I know, Mrs Kerr, always taken a keen – one could say almost reverential – interest in the school which your late husband started with such initiative forty years ago."

"Almost forty," Julia corrected him.

He bowed. "And as a Guild we, since our inception, have backed you."

"Really?"

"Forgive me, backed you as far as we were able. We have sent students to you when any came our way, and we have always, as you will agree, worked together amicably."

"Of course, yes. Naturally. Why not?"

"Hmm. Well – the fact of the matter is, Mrs Kerr, I will be blunt – a meeting of our Guild was held last night to discuss certain aspects of art in Port Todric which have become worrying to say the least lately. And the general opinion reached was that a united attack should be made on a certain section of our community."

"Meaning?"

"In the name of art, all that it has stood for in the past and

136

its future in Port Todric, we are asking you to stand with us and bar from your school those young people who at present are blackening the name of artists in the eyes of decent citizens."

"But – but – do you mean – are you asking me to *expel* students?" queried Julia.

"Those who are detrimental to the community, yes," Ainsworths answered.

"What community? Art?"

"Society as a whole," he stated pompously.

Until then Julia herself had mostly supported the Guild on artistic matters. But Ainsworth's present attitude now – his bigotry, and assurance that she would comply with his utterly impossible suggestion – almost forced her to the other camp.

"I can't do that. Of course I can't. This school has never been sponsored by one particular group of artists. The idea's quite unthinkable."

"You realise, I suppose," Ainsworth said smoothly, "that at the present moment, unless you change your tactics, what identity your group has will be completely swamped and lost."

"What do you mean?"

His right eyebrow shot up. "Kent's influence is not good. He favours the type of student we'd rather keep away. In any case, Mrs Kerr, I should have thought that merely on moral grounds – "

"Mr Ainsworth!" Julia's eyes flashed. "The Stephen Kerr School was never inaugurated as a school of morals, and I don't propose to change its policy at this late date. True, my husband had a definite technique – a style of his own – which I have tried to keep alive since his death. But in ideas the group was always free-thinking; he left the student alone as much as possible to follow his own individual trend. Stephen would have been the last person to send anyone away simply because his conception of painting differed from his own, or because he had different standards of living. The only yardstick was merit. As a matter of fact, I admire some of the modern work quite a bit, and persona! morality doesn't come into it. So please let us end this stupid conversation."

There was a pause while Ainsworth fidgeted with his tie and swallowed hard to smother his annoyance. Then he remarked, "We should be grateful to think you were with us in the matter, Mrs Kerr, and I'm sure when you've thought it over carefully you'll agree that in the past we've been of *some* help to you?"

"Certainly. But on the other hand, Mr Ainsworth, the school has been of assistance to you also."

"True, quite true," he agreed. "That's why I'm sure you'll consider very carefully before you turn down what is a practical, as well as an aesthetic and spiritual suggestion."

Spiritual! The little snob! Feeling the blood mounting in her cheeks, Julia said quickly, "If you mean about the students, Mr Ainsworth, I shan't reconsider anything. I'm sorry you troubled to come and see me if that was the only reason."

Richard Ainsworth was picking up his gloves, on the point of going, when there was another knock at the door, revealing Kent on the step. For a second she felt nonplussed, then the irony of the situation struck her and she began to enjoy herself.

"Hullo," she said. "I didn't expect you. Come in."

Without appearing to, she noted the perceptible stiffening of Ainsworth's form, caught the distaste for each other which flashed momentarily into the two men's eyes. Then Richard Ainsworth gave his short characteristic little bow and said briefly, "Good evening." Nothing more.

Kent made a similar gesture.

"A lovely night," he said.

"Perfect," the older man agreed. Then he extended his hand in farewell to Julia.

"But need you go?" she said mischievously. "I'm sure there's quite a lot we three could still discuss together."

Annoyance twitched the pointed beard and eyebrows. "I'm afraid I'm in rather a hurry, Mrs Kerr. But I hope you'll think over what I've said."

They said goodnight formally, and a moment later Julia was facing Kent across the table.

He drew out his cigarette case.

She took one, and he lit it for her in silence. Then he said, "What did that little bounder want?"

138

"Oh, I should hardly call him a bounder," Julia said. "Mr Ainsworth is a very principled man." She smiled to herself.

Kent frowned. "You know, Mrs Kerr," he said, "I don't think it's possible to go on much longer with a foot in each camp."

"What do you mean?"

"I don't know what Ainsworth's object was in coming to see you, and I don't imagine you'll tell me."

"Quite right," she agreed affably.

"But it's pretty clear," he went on, "that he's out to make trouble. He's nothing more than a dictator. After all, Port Todric doesn't belong to him, but he wants it to. Ainsworth and his crowd want to rule the roost, simply because they're afraid of competition, afraid of any new ideas cutting into their stick-in-the-mud theories."

Julia sighed. "Just what *do* you mean? I've never before been embroiled in such ridiculous competition. In the last two months or so a nasty, perfectly childish, atmosphere of rivalry seems to have sprung up between the artists. But it's not going to happen in the Stephen Kerr School. I've just said so in so many words to Ainsworth, and – "

"So I was right."

She waved her hand impatiently. "That's entirely beside the point. You're both as bad as each other. As for the work – while I'm here the school will go on with the policy it's always had: merit only. I certainly don't intend cutting myself from either group. Actually I'm beginning to wonder if it wouldn't be best, after all, to close the studio."

"Close it?"

"Perhaps not yet," she admitted. "But while it's in Stephen's name, Kent, don't come to me with petty whims and squabbling. And I mean that."

His temper rose. "You may be in for a nasty shock. The situation's unhealthy, and I shouldn't be surprised myself if one or two slander actions don't appear on the scene yet."

"That will be unfortunate," Julia said equably. "Slander actions generally leave such a nasty taste in the mouth."

Kent left soon afterwards, leaving Julia feeling tired and depressed. Whilst the battle went on she could keep her end up, but afterwards she couldn't help realising what a senseless waste of energy it all was.

I suppose a great deal of it comes down to a queer kind of fear, she thought, making herself a cup of tea. Ainsworth and his cronies are frightened that the opposite group may steal their thunder where publicity's concerned, which could affect sales. Kent and his followers are fighting to get established, and nervous that the others are going to put a spoke in their wheel. Oh, dear, why can't they work together? We need standards, but we need the young, too. What Stephen would have thought I don't know.

But then Stephen, with his charm and tact, would probably have managed better. Stephen would have accepted no different camps, he would have managed somehow to be beloved in both. She had probably muddled the whole thing by making both Ainsworth and Kent dislike her. If she'd been more diplomatic . . . but she was first and foremost a fighter, and the years of struggling on alone had increased that capacity in her.

The next few months were significant in the history of Port Todric art. Somehow a correspondence between the rival groups was started in the local press, which involved a certain amount of mud-slinging, and was, Julia thought, altogether deplorable. Saner members on either side detached themselves and resigned. Kent himself, now quite open in his tactics, was in the forefront of the war.

I shall have to get rid of him, Julia thought. And who to get instead I just don't know.

Sarah, meanwhile, wrote enthusiastic letters concerning her life at college.

> Next year I may have a shot for the Darrant Medal.
> Then if I got it there'd be some sort of grant, and the
> publicity would be jolly good, too. I don't suppose
> there's much chance really but Mr Geen – you know,
> the master I told you about – thinks I ought to try. It
> would be great, wouldn't it, if I could pull it off?

Peter, who came over to see Julia shortly after she had received this letter, was not so enthusiastic.

"Of course I want Sarah to do well," he said dubiously.

140

"But, dash it all, Mrs Kerr, I love her. If she gets too embroiled in a career, what will happen to me?"

"You mustn't try to clip her wings," Julia told him. "If Sarah really cares for you she won't let her work stand in the way. And you know she isn't just an ordinary kind of girl – "

"That's true," he agreed grudgingly. "What she sees in me, heaven only knows."

"She sees what any intelligent girl would see," Julia answered. "A thoroughly nice person, and a good husband-to-be. And I'm sure she loves you too, but she's very young, and restless. This isn't a fad of hers. From being a little girl Sarah's had what most of us haven't – a streak of genius. Yes, I'm sure of it. I'm not exaggerating. And it would be wrong to stifle it. Not only wrong, but impossible. You've got to realise that before you're married – to realise and respect it. Then – well, I think you've every chance of being happy."

"Thank you. I don't want to stand in her way. I'm interested in her sculpting, so long as it doesn't divide us."

"That's your problem. And don't frown, I'm sure you're up to it."

Sarah was to return for the holidays at the beginning of August. Shortly before the date of her arrival, Julia had an unexpected visitor. David Blair arrived one afternoon when she was just preparing tea. She started when she saw him there on the doorstep. Momentary shock made her pause before asking him in. She was trembling slightly, already on the defensive for Sarah and Stephen. Yet what harm could he do them? They were grown up. It was hardly likely at this point he'd risk saying anything to discredit himself or Caroline in their eyes. Steadying herself, she scrutinised him closely. He'd changed as so many men of his type did with middle age. His good looks had coarsened, he was stouter, a little dissipated-looking. His fawnish eyes had the tired disillusioned look of one who'd lived not wisely but too well. He appeared also a little confused, hesitant, although behind it all the insolent charm was there. Despite herself Julia saw a vestige of that appeal which years ago had swayed Caroline to such excess. She had never liked him, and had no illusions about him now. But politeness allied to a certain odd curiosity checked any display of hostility from her. He re-introduced himself ironically, was at first guarded, then, as tension between them slackened, said more easily, "I suppose you're wondering why I've come?"

"Naturally."

"You know, of course," he continued, after a pause, "of the very deep – friendship once existing between your daughter and myself?"

"That was a very long time ago." Her voice was aloof, cool.

"Nearly twenty years," he agreed, "so explanations at this point are perhaps unnecessary?"

"Well, they can hardly do any good."

"No. To no one but myself."

"And could do harm to others."

"Caroline's children? Oh, surely not. In any case, I'm exerting no rights. But I'm naturally interested."

"Isn't it rather late in the day to rake up old relationships? What good does it do? Even if your interest is justified."

"And you *know* it is, don't you?"

"Mr Blair, I admit nothing. I've the children – *mine* – to think of. And as I was saying – what good?"

"I should like to do something. For the girl, anyway," he said bluntly.

"Oh. The girl."

"As a friend, nothing more unless you agree. I'm in a position now to – "

"As a friend," she interrupted, "I couldn't stop you. But I should have thought the whole matter was too painful to resurrect."

"Need we fence?" he said. "*You* know and *I* know that those children are mine. Do you think I should come here at all if it wasn't for their benefit?"

"Remembering the past," Julia said, "I don't know what you'd do. And I'm not sure that I trust you. Legally, you know – "

"Oh, legally!" he said with a short laugh of contempt. "Don't worry, I know I haven't a leg to stand on. And why should I want it?"

"What is it you *do* want?"

"As you say, I can do what I like for them in the capacity of a friend, and I'm willing to become and remain that friend –

nothing more – providing you have no objection to my seeing them when there's an opportunity."

"But what opportunity is there?" Julia said quickly. "Surely you're not intending to stay in Port Todric? Sarah happens to be in London studying at the moment, Stephen's at sea. And I don't see that any good could come of an arranged meeting."

"Nor any harm either," Blair remarked shortly. "As they happen to be my children – in blood if not name – wanting to meet them's not an abnormal request. I've assured you that I'll say nothing, provided you're reasonable."

"I see. Blackmail."

"Oh, hardly that."

"I don't know what else you'd call it," Julia said tartly.

"Well, I don't mean it that way," he assured her, smiling. "Natural interest, no more."

"Somewhat delayed."

He had the grace to flush slightly. There was a pause after which he resumed, "Well?"

Julia thought quickly. "All right. On your conditions. Sarah, I mean. There's no knowing when Stephen will be home. But Sarah returns next week."

"Thank you."

"You can come to tea," she went on, without emotion. "Or, no – better still – we'll meet out."

Before he left they arranged a date. Julia, still confused, was not sure whether or not she had handled the situation wisely. But although she didn't like Blair she felt confident that he would stick to the bargain. Whereas if she'd denied him the opportunity, he might have resorted to more compromising means, and would certainly have no respect for her feelings.

And so, a week later, Julia and Sarah met Blair one afternoon outside the Blue Teapot. Sarah, in a simply cut blue woollen frock with a small felt hat of the same colour, was looking very nice, Julia thought, and was admirably self-possessed, although her eyes held a faint probing puzzled look, as though she did not fully understand why they should be meeting this man who, those years ago, Julia had so obviously avoided. Still, he seemed nicer now. Older and kinder somehow, and he *did* seem interested in her work. That was good. So many men, Sarah had discovered, treated a woman's career as something mildly amusing which could never seriously matter.

"You just let me know if you do get that medal," Blair said once, with his strange long eyes so like her own upon her. "And I expect you will."

She shook her head and laughed. "Oh, no, that's not at all certain. I've not really been studying long enough. But if I do pull it off it'll be just marvellous. Not just because of the honour of it and everything, but you see I'm going to be married, and I do want Peter to understand that my work matters. Then I'll be able to go on with it, and well, that's how it is," she concluded, still smiling.

"Married?" Blair said, with a questioning look at Julia. "Oh, I see. You didn't tell me."

"I never thought," Julia said. "But, yes, Sarah and Peter have been engaged for some months."

"And what does he do? Is he an artist?"

"Oh, no, a farmer. I met him when I was on the land."

"But my dear girl, *you* can't be a farmer's wife – milking, working all day, spoiling your hands."

"Oh, it isn't that kind of farm," Sarah explained. "It's very large, and I shan't spoil my hands, that's all fixed."

"Well, I hope you'll let me meet this young man of yours one day."

Sarah's eyes brightened. "Of course," she said enthusiastically. "You must come over to Poldragon some time, Peter would be glad."

Julia frowned. This was not what she had planned at all. But after Sarah had gone some time later, he said to Julia before leaving her, "Don't worry, a bargain's a bargain. I shan't let the cat out of the bag. In any case, I wouldn't upset the child. I like her. She's just the sort of daughter I'd have liked to have around."

Julia made no reply. She really didn't know whether she'd acted for the best or not in letting him into their lives at all. But he *was* the girl's father, she'd never doubted that, and however despicably Blair had behaved in the past she supposed there were certain moral claims. So she put worry from her, and returned to the flat to what she hoped would be a quiet evening. But in this she was disappointed.

When she got back she found that as usual on a Friday the weekly edition of the local paper had been pushed through the letterbox. She picked it up from the mat, and when she'd removed her hat and coat, took it to her favourite chair and sat down. She scanned it quickly, ending with the letters column. Something there caught her eye. Something which made her start, before continuing to read. There under the heading "Local Art School in Conflict" was a letter from Kent.

It began with a sarcastic reference to the activities of the Painters' Guild phrased in no uncertain terms, and went on:

As tutor at the Stephen Kerr School which was founded on progressive lines, I feel a point has come in the history of art at Port Todric when its policy should be made quite clear. This school has never been under the dictates of an effete and bigoted group such as that run by a handful of old men and women who at the moment are endeavouring to check progress and have art scheduled in this town as a kindergarten for imbeciles, allowing themselves to be gulled purely for commercial ends. I mention no names. But let it be understood that I for one do not allow my name to be used in any capacity concerned with the Painters' Guild.

Yours truly,
Richard Kent

For some moments Julia sat quite still with the offensive letter in front of her. Then a slow, dull crimson suffused her cheeks. She stood up. The impudence of it! Oh, the impudence. The letter was not only slanderous, it was insolent to her. It would damage all that Stephen had sought to build up, bringing the school itself into a vulgar brawl.

Indignantly, wasting no time, she pulled on a loose cape and went out. She found Kent in his studio, daubing at what appeared to be a topsy-turvy landscape, childlike, out-of-perspective, lacking all the accepted merits of straightforward good painting.

145

He turned his head. "Oh. Do come in."

Chin lifted, two bright spots of colour in her face, she strode forward waving the paper.

"Oh, I see. Well?" He waited.

"Well! You may well say '*well*'! What about it? What *about* this?"

He laughed humourlessly. "I don't understand."

"This paragraph – you wrote it obviously. It's in your name."

"I don't know why you're so agitated, Mrs Kerr," Kent said after a moment. "Something had to be done, and for my part I'm relieved to see it in print. Maybe it'll stop the antics that have been going on."

"Stop?" Julia said scornfully. "You must be mad. Do you realise this could be actionable? Another thing. It's against everything we've stood for. You've gone beyond your right."

"I don't see it," Kent said stubbornly. "I'm entitled to my views, and just because I happen to be working for your precious school doesn't mean that I've got to sit by like any nitwit and let that lot get away with their sly games."

"You've brought the group into it," Julia went on. "*Stephen's* school."

"Oh, for God's sake," Kent put in impatiently, "do have a sense of perspective. It's in your own interests. Surely you don't want the place to become a laughing stock?"

"That's what you've made it already," Julia retorted grimly. "And I'm really tired of it – just tired. And I mean it."

"The same goes for me."

"So there's only one thing to be done, isn't there? You'd better go. Leave – in your own interests as well as mine."

"You needn't tell me," he answered. "I'd already made up my mind."

"You can take a month's salary," she broke in, "and take your notice as from today."

His eyes flashed. "If I were you, I'd be careful," he said, "I can smash the Stephen Kerr School, make no mistake about it."

She laughed. "Such heroics. What do you think you can do? It will take more than one man to break up this school, Mr Kent. You're behaving quite ridiculously."

146

"And you," he said, "are acting like a fishwife."

She stared at him. "*Kent*!"

"You're a stupid woman," he said, "just a stupid woman. And I wonder I've stuck it so long."

She turned to go. "Well, we'll see about the stupidity," she said more quietly. "You've insulted me and I shan't forget it."

When she got outside again, she found ridiculously that her knees were trembling, and her heart was beating more painfully than it should against her sides. She steadied herself, and went. At the corner of the road she met Sarah.

"Why, Nan," the girl said, "what's the matter? You look all out of breath."

"That man," Julia panted, "Kent. He's upset me. I'm getting rid of him, Sarah. He's no good."

Sarah took her arm. "Don't worry. He never was. I never liked him. I shouldn't bother about *him*."

"Oh, but it's more than that," Julia replied. "It's the school, Sarah, the harm he's done. This letter in the paper. You don't understand."

She laughed. "The row, you mean. Oh, but who'll take any notice of that? It's been going on for ages anyhow, and everybody laughs about it."

"That's just it. The Stephen Kerr School."

"Well, you can put that all right. Why don't you write something yourself?"

Yes, why not? It was an idea.

The following week a letter from Julia herself appeared in the press. It was brief and to the point.

I should like anyone who is at all interested in the Stephen Kerr School to understand that Mr Kent is no longer concerned in any way with its activities. In a letter last week certain references were made which in no way uphold its principles. The school takes no part in the rivalry of different groups. Its one concern is to teach good art to any having the necessary qualifications. And it is with great regret that the school should have been brought into discussions which do not concern it.

Yours truly,
Julia Kerr

After Kent's exit Julia herself once more started the daily jaunt to the studio. Spurred on by her challenge to Kent, by her unflagging will to keep the school going at any cost, she did not in those few months feel her sixty-three years. Neither did she look it. Though her hair was greying now, her carriage was still good, her figure erect. The lines of her face had not changed much. There were days when in a certain light and a certain posture the Julia of her youth was still there. Her quick temper was the same, and she had still the capacity for a good fight.

I am an old woman, she thought one day, but I think Stephen would still recognise me. And she smiled, remembering the tussles they had had.

At first she had wondered whether Kent would make a fuss over her note in the press. But she need not have feared, for in that same month Kerr was confronted by a solicitor's letter on behalf of the Guild which threatened him with legal action unless he did not immediately withdraw his statements concerning the abusive phrases relating to members of the group.

"I'm damned if I will," Kent said when the communication arrived. He didn't really believe that his letter was actionable, since no individual had been personally named. He was dismayed therefore when his own solicitor advised him to make the necessary apology.

"As a public body they may actually go to court," he was told. "And a case of this kind doesn't always necessitate actual names. If I were you I would write the letter. After all, you might win but on the other hand you may be let in for damages. Is it worth it?"

No. On thinking it over, Kent decided that it wasn't. But I'll get even with Julia Kerr, he decided. Yes, in one way or another I will.

Julia could not help being aware of Kent's increasing hostility. She noticed, too, that since his dismissal he appeared to be going to seed, was untidy in appearance, and was known to be drinking too much. This worried her; she didn't like to think herself in any way responsible for a man's downfall. Then commonsense reasserted itself. After all, he'd brought it upon himself. It was not her doing.

One evening she returned late from the studio feeling, for once, quite tired out by the class. She realised, turning the corner of the street, that she could not go on as she was doing indefinitely. She would have to get someone else. It had begun all over again then, the old search for an assistant. Not only annoying, but exhausting.

Occupied by her own thoughts she did not notice, until she was almost at the entrance to 7a, a figure slouched against the steps. Drawing nearer she saw with surprise that it was Kent, his chin sunk into his collar, his hat pushed forward over his eyes. Clearly he had been drinking. Professing not to notice him she pushed by with a curt, "Excuse me." But he lurched forward, blocking her way.

"Evening," he said, "want to see you."

"I think you must be mistaken," Julia stated. "Please get out of my way."

"Want to see you," he repeated. "Urgent – very urgent."

"Oh, Kent, pull yourself together," Julia said sharply. "You'll cause a commotion."

"Don't care if I do," he said truculently. "Must – must see you."

Julia thought quickly. "What about?"

"Tell you later," he answered.

"You're in no state to talk," she said, "and I've nothing to say to you."

"No, but *I* have," he said, with more decision. "Yes, I've something t'say t'*you.*"

"If you don't let me pass," Julia said firmly, "I'll call the police."

"Oh, no, no, don't call the police, make such a jolly awful row – everyone talk – "

That was true. Julia decided to take another line.

"Look here, Kent," she said more kindly, "please go home now. I'm tired tonight. Tomorrow, if the matter's so urgent, I'll meet you to see what you have to say – "

"No, no good. Now," he insisted. "*Now.* Why not? I'm not – I'm not really so drunk as all that, you know."

He did seem to have sobered up a little. So on a foolish impulse, and to save a scene, she said abruptly, "Very well, come in. But you must be quick about it. My granddaughter's

149

gone to the pictures and will be back shortly. I don't want her to run into any unpleasant argument."

"No argument," he said, "why should there be?"

He followed her inside, and once in the lounge flopped down into a chair.

"Now," Julia said, "what is it? Please explain. I shan't offer you a drink. You've obviously had more than enough. It's a pity you're letting yourself go."

"And whose fault's that?" His voice was sullen.

"Your own," she told him harshly.

"Ha! I like that. Pushing a man out of his job, kicking him when he's down. Bloody mean, I call it."

"You forget yourself."

"Always the same, aren't you? Hard as nails. Always was. Always."

"Kent! If that's all you've got to tell me, I think you'd better go."

"Maybe you do. But I won't, see? Time someone told you what they thought of you. Glad it's me." He chuckled.

Julia looked disgusted. "You're quite drunk. I was a fool to let you in."

"Right, quite right. Damn fool. 'Cos now I shan't go till I want to."

Julia glared at him icily. "We'll see about that. It won't take me long to 'phone the police." She made as if to get up.

He jumped up, clutching her arm wildly. She stepped back, freeing herself. "Don't you dare touch me."

He laughed again. "Why not? Bit passé, perhaps, but not so bad in the dark."

Julia, white-faced, lifted her arm and brought her hand down in a stinging blow across his face.

He reeled back into the chair, covering his face with his hands. "Oh my God! Oh, God!"

Her lip curled contemptuously. "Be quiet."

He looked up at her, and she was shocked by the expression of sheer despair she saw there. It was more than hatred or misery or rage, it was stark, unmitigated despair.

"A fool," he said, "that's what I am – a fool. Just a poor damn fool. Fool to think a woman like you could have pity or understanding. *Pity*? That look in your eyes! Seen it on men's

150

faces in the war. Ruthless – the killing look. Yes. If it was to save your blasted school you could put a bullet through me soon as wink your eye. I know your sort. That's why I'm here now, like this, without a job, without credentials – all because of the school, *his* school – Stephen K-Kerr's."

Julia, with one hand on her breast, watched him as his eyes slid round to the large life-size self-portrait of Stephen painted the year before his death, which was hanging over the mantelpiece.

"That's it," Kent went on wildly, "that's it – the school. Everything for the school. Men don't matter, souls don't matter. Only the school."

He was silent for a few moments, a pause in which Julia racked her brains for an idea, some course of action that would put an end to the distressing scene.

But a few moments later he was off again.

"That's why wars happen – same thing. Ideology! State, school – all the same. I hate your school. I *hate* it, I tell you."

He rose unsteadily to his feet again, swerving towards the portrait. But until he was close upon it Julia did not realise his intention. Then, in a sickening instant, she saw him reach wildly for her pair of scissors on the shelf, and plunge them once, twice, several times, into the canvas, ripping it in several places.

There was silence. She could hear Kent breathing heavily. Then she saw him wipe his brow with his handkerchief, and slowly turn round. He was very pale.

"There. That's done. Good job. An end of it. End of Stephen Kerr School. Yes, I'm glad."

Julia said nothing. He sat down, shaking, and when still she did not speak, looked up and said, "Get the police if you like. Don't care any more. Not now, not now it's done. Well – get it over, can't you?"

Julia shook her head slowly. "You poor thing," she said. "You poor, poor thing."

A gleam of bewilderment lit Kent's blurred eyes. "I don't understand. Aren't you – aren't you going to get them?"

"No. What's the good? Why should I?"

"But – the painting."

"Yes. You've finished that."

151

"Don't you care, then?" He was frankly puzzled.

Julia hid her eyes wearily. "Yes, I care. But, after all, it's only a portrait. The real Stephen – " She broke off, looked up and continued after a moment, "The real Stephen's stronger than that."

Kent dropped his head into his hands again. She stood watching him, and so they remained silent until he stirred, lumbered to his feet and said, "I'll be going."

She shook her head. "You can't go in that state. You'd better stay here. Sarah will be back at any moment. We'll rig you up for the night."

She could hardly have done less, she thought wearily later, as Sarah helped her prepare the sofa. Her anger had indeed all gone. She was aware only of a profound pity tinged with a mild contempt. Had she done wrong, she wondered, to sack him in the way she had? But surely this last scene was but proof of the man's complete unsuitability for the post?

Sarah was indignant.

"I don't know why on earth you kept him here," she said, when they had gone to bed leaving Kent sleeping on the couch, "a rotter like that. *I* wouldn't, I'd have got the police."

Julia sighed. "It's not so simple as that, Sarah. He's never been really well since the war, and I should have known better than to have taken him on in the first instance. One must be as kind as possible, I suppose, but what's going to happen to him I can't think."

"Well, that's not our affair," Sarah said, still indignantly. "So, Nan, please don't go thinking it is. I know you. You pretend to be hard one moment, and all the time you're shaking like a jelly with sentiment underneath."

Julia was mildly annoyed. "Don't talk like that, Sarah. I know what I'm doing."

The next day Kent woke shamefaced and apologetic, but his apologies had a tinge of irony in them, and Julia knew that he resented being indebted to her. He looked ill, but pulled himself together with a show of bravado as he left.

"Sorry and all that," he said, "can hardly say I hope to do the same for you one day, can I?"

"Hardly," Julia agreed. "But take yourself in hand, Kent, you've got brains and talent, if you really use them."

"Thanks," he smiled mockingly. "But brains in this world can be damn' inconvenient."

She was glad he had returned to mockery. This fact relieved her of any remaining sense of responsibility in his welfare.

For the next few weeks Julia was kept busy at the studio, interviewing various applicants for the post, most of whom were completely unsuitable.

Then, the day after Sarah had returned to London, a young man presented himself, fully trained, with excellent credentials, whose name, he said, was La Roche. He had been born in Canada, he told her, of half-French parentage, but had come to England to study art in 1934. In the war he had served with the air force, and now wished to resume his career. He showed her specimens of his work, chiefly water colours, which impressed her with their freshness and spontaneity. He was very charming, dark, with an attractive teasing smile, and had she been a younger woman she might have fallen for him without reserve. As it was, she liked him, although a lingering doubt remained in her mind, even when she had taken him on. And yet there was no reason for that doubt, she told herself, nothing tangible at all. It was just, perhaps, that he was a trifle too charming for safety.

However, as the first few weeks passed he proved himself completely successful in the job, and by October she felt that at last she could relax, the problem solved, and the Stephen Kerr School on its feet again.

Chapter Twenty-One

Christmas came, and was marked for Julia by a tragic event resulting in Kent's death. Of recent months he had seemed to take hold of himself, working hard at his own painting and holding an exhibition at which he sold several of his landscapes. It was the more ironic therefore that the end should come just then, when Julia was telling herself that everything had worked out for the best – not only for herself but for the former tutor. His fall from a cliff one night, when he was on one of his late wanderings – a habit formed since he had left the school – seemed to mark for her the ending of another chapter, although she had seen very little of him in the recent weeks. His death was presumed to be accidental, but Julia could not force from her mind the haunting possibility that an inner despair had forced the issue.

When spring came, however, her spirits rose, and letters from Sarah further cheered her. She was full of optimism concerning the medal. The sending-in date was in May, and she told Julia that by June the results should be known.

"Of course it may not come off," she wrote, "but I've got every hope, Nan. Geen thinks I shall get it. Isn't it thrilling? My main piece is going to be called 'The Beginning'; it's supposed to be the conception of everything, groping figures evolving from the earth. I expect it sounds rather ambitious and a bit silly on paper, but I'm terribly excited about it. By the way, I had a long letter from Mr Blair. He's really rather nice, I think. Peter quite liked him, and when he comes to town to see me, we're all three going to meet."

Julia's feelings were mixed on the subject of Blair.

However, if he was going to behave himself – and she rather thought he was – no harm could come of it. Indeed, if he took a genuine interest in Sarah it might even be to her advantage. She was not sure of Peter's financial position; the upkeep of Poldragon must be considerable, and there would not be much coming to Sarah when she, Julia, was gone. It seemed hardly sense therefore to look a gift-horse in the mouth.

So, in this sanguine mood, time passed until one day an upsetting incident occurred. She had turned into a cafe for a cup of coffee following a morning's shopping and had the misfortune to encounter Jane Anderson, a student of the group. Miss Anderson, rather fussy and middle-aged but a clever painter of flowers, had been attending now for three years, and although Julia was not personally very interested in her work, politeness induced her to make room for her at her own table. Conversation quickly veered towards matters concerning the Stephen Kerr School, including the new tutor.

"Oh, that young Mr La Roche is *charming*," Miss Anderson said presently. "Absolutely. And clever, too. Much cleverer than that poor Kent." Then her voice dropped. "It seems a pity that – "

Her words trailed off, and Julia looked up.

"Yes?"

"Well, of course, I mean to say, it's none of my business but – "

A frown creased Julia's forehead. "But what, Miss Anderson? If it's anything to do with the school . . ."

"Oh, I'm not sure it *is*," the other woman went on. "At least, I mean, not definitely. But of course things get about."

"Miss Anderson, please do tell me what it's all about. Is it something to do with Mr La Roche?"

Jane Anderson looked uncomfortable. "I'm afraid it is, Mrs Kerr. Possibly you won't think it very important, but he *is* rather friendly with that new little model, Sally Talland."

A little gasp of astonishment left Julia's lips. "Friendly? But of course he's friendly. She works there. They could hardly not be."

Miss Anderson's lips tightened. "I hardly meant that. The

truth is, they're having an affair, and there *are* rumours that the previous model had to leave the town."

"What do you mean?"

"Oh, please don't be annoyed, Mrs Kerr. But it's better you should know. They say she had a baby, and that it was his – La Roche's."

Julia laughed. "But that's ridiculous. Why, he was hardly ever with her. I can't believe – "

"That's just it," Miss Anderson said primly. "That's what makes it so disgraceful. The secrecy. You see, Mr Vane saw them leaving one night, very late, about one o'clock. They'd been in the studio all that time together, and now this other affair on top of it and the same thing happening. Well! I'm afraid the school may get a bad name. Of course, I know it's nothing to do with *you*, but – "

"If the school is involved in any scandal, it's certainly my affair," Julia said shortly. "And I'll look into it, of course, if only on La Roche's account. After all, if such rumours are going about it's very bad for him as well as for myself. I'm glad you told me, but I don't believe it. It seems to me quite unheard of. Mere malicious gossip. I can't imagine it of him for one moment, and I think Mr Vane should have told me in the first place before spreading unfounded scandalous rumours."

"Oh, please don't blame Mr Vane," Miss Anderson said, looking distressed. "He's old, you know, and rather shy. He wouldn't like to think of upsetting you. Besides, Mr Vane is not the only one, oh, no – not by any means."

Julia's spirits were low when half an hour later she returned home. She told herself still that the matter was merely one of malicious gossip, but the lingering doubt she had had about La Roche when she first engaged him returned with renewed force. His love affairs were his own business. But if it was true – if he was 'carrying on' with the girl at late hours in the studio – then the matter became the responsibility of the school, and it was up to her to put a stop to it. She was dismayed by the thought, dreading the possibility of having to dismiss him which would mean the dreary search again for a suitable replacement.

For several days she did nothing about it, but in the same

week she met Sally Talland by chance at the corner of Crab Street. She was rather a pretty girl, with a pale heart-shaped face and very light blonde hair falling to her shoulders. Her expression on the whole was sulky and inclined to insolence, but Julia put this down to the fact that she did not have a happy home life. Her father, a local man of the strictest religious principles, had died five years ago, leaving Sally, who was then twelve, to the care of a bad-tempered slatternly stepmother, his second wife. Julia had been glad to take the girl on, because she knew that the wages she earned saved her from the harsh treatment that had been too frequent a portion of her childhood. The suggestion that La Roche might have taken advantage of the situation was worrying in the extreme.

"Well, Sally," Julia enquired, determined to find out what she could from this encounter, "and how are you getting on at the school? Still like it?"

"Oh, yes, it's all right," the girl replied ambiguously.

"And Mr La Roche? Do you get on with him?"

"Yes," Sally replied, with a sidelong glance – almost sly – from her slant eyes, "he's O.K."

"You get home punctually, don't you?" Julia pursued. "You're not expected to work overtime, you know."

"I don't. Why should I?"

"Oh, nothing. But sometimes, when artists get too immersed in their paintings, they forget time and just go ahead, not realising how late it is."

"Well, he don't," Sally replied sullenly. "And why you should think so I don't know. What's it matter what time I go home anyhow?"

"Of course it doesn't," Julia replied equably. "But it's my business to see that things are going on as they should for you. I was merely enquiring."

"I've told you, it's all right."

Julia wasn't satisfied. Her conversation with Sally had increased rather than allayed her fears. She might have appeared a 'busy-body' to the girl – times were changing and old values seemed to be on the wane – but she, Julia, had to speak her mind.

She brooded over the matter for the weekend and on the Monday decided that the time had come for her to take definite action, to see for herself whether or not the rumours were true.

At nine o'clock, when she'd had her evening meal, she slipped on her coat and went over to the school. She was tense and a little breathless when she arrived at the studio but at her first glance of the locked door and closed windows, something of her anxiety subsided. Obviously he was not there. It was a particularly still night, and there was no sound of movement from within.

She went forward, and inserted her key softly into the door. Then, very quietly, she went up the stairs, pausing at the top for a moment before opening the inner door. A cat scudded through the dying light into the shadows. But beyond that no sight or sound of activity broke the silence. She drew a breath of relief and went on into the room. Then, to her dismay, there came the faint sound of scuffling in one corner. The cat, of course, it *must* be the cat, she thought as her heart quickened. But the next minute she knew her mistake. That was no cat – the sudden glimpse of white, of figures moving, half-hidden by the screen.

"What are you doing?" Julia called harshly, in a half whisper. "Who's that?"

She switched on her torch, and in its beam saw a girl struggling to dress herself. At the same moment a man rose to his feet, smiling shamefacedly, and striving for dignity.

"Only me, Mrs Kerr," she heard La Roche saying lightly. "Working late tonight, been doing a little to my painting."

"Light the lamp." Disgust froze Julia's voice.

"Certainly."

La Roche crossed to the table and did so. By that time Sally was dressed in a fashion, and standing defiantly by him. A suspender belt, none too clean, lay on the floor, and her hair was still ruffled about her shoulders.

"Now," Julia's voice was deadly, "what does this all mean?"

"The poor child was tired," La Roche said, prevaricating. "Resting, that's all."

"I see. And when have the terms of our agreement allowed you to carry on affairs with your mistresses after hours?"

La Roche laughed unpleasantly. "Come now, Mrs Kerr,

aren't you making rather a lot out of nothing? It *is* late, I agree, but – "

"Of course," Julia continued, "I know the French have different standards of morality, but I should have thought even you would have stopped short of seduction on my premises."

"You've no proof of it. You should be careful, madame."

"Tch! I have every proof. The whole school knows. But until this moment I was too blind to believe it."

"Well, damn it all, I've done *you* no harm."

"If you injure the school you injure me. And this girl's employed by me. You've behaved despicably." She turned to Sally. "Straighten your hair, and finish dressing."

"Leave me alone."

"Do as I say. *Please*."

"Look here!" La Roche's voice was shrill. "She is not your property, to order about."

"I should keep quiet if I were you," Julia retorted icily. "It's my business to see she gets home as quickly as possible, and I mean to do so."

The girl edged away. "No, no, I'm not going, see, I'm not going there."

"Why not?"

"She'll only get beaten," La Roche said coolly. "Do you realise what a hell of a home she's got?"

"Which you're only making worse. Unless, of course, you intend to do the honourable thing by marrying her. But I hardly think that's your role, is it?" Knowing how melodramatic she sounded, Julia realised from the expression on La Roche's face that her words had made their point. For a moment a flash of fear mingled with dislike crossed the cold countenance. "You see," she said to the girl, "what he thinks of you. Now you hurry up and come with me. We'll see about your mother later."

"No, I won't."

"Oh, yes you will, even if I have to drag you. As for you, La Roche, don't let me see your face in the studio again. And if this girl comes to any harm, I shall know who's responsible."

He gave a short contemptuous laugh, and at the door turned. She saw incredulously that he seemed genuinely

159

amused, although it may have been a pose, mere bravado to save his own face.

"Mon dieu, Mrs Kerr," he said, "you're quite funny. All this ballyhoo over a kiss in the dark. I always heard the English were repressed. Now I know it. Goodnight."

He bowed, turned, there was a short click of the door, and he was gone. Julia turned to Sally.

"Well, are you ready?"

"I hate you," Sally said, between anger and tears. "You've spoiled everything, you interfering old busybody."

Julia's eyes were grim. "Enough of that, Sally. Here, take your coat, and hurry up. It's late."

"I'm not going."

"You *are* coming. And if you get beaten it'll be your own fault. You deserve it."

The girl began to cry. "Oh, no, no, I can't go home. It's awful, I'd kill myself rather."

Seeing that she was on the verge of hysterics, Julia softened. "If you behave reasonably, maybe I'll go and see your stepmother myself. You can come back with me tonight. But no more scenes, understand?"

Sally pulled herself together and dried her eyes. "All right," she said sulkily after a moment. "I'll come."

Trailing along with her through the darkness, Julia wondered ironically if a time would ever arrive when she was not somehow to be embroiled in other people's affairs. But perhaps it was her own fault, perhaps she was a born meddler.

My home seems to be nothing more than a refuge for lame ducks, she thought, a little ruefully, turning up Crab Street. Still, that's something, I suppose.

When she'd got Sally installed she went off alone to find the woman concerned. The interview was easier but in some ways more unpleasant than she'd expected, probably due to the empty gin bottle on the untidy living room table. The sounds of a man's snoring came from the other room. A check cap lay on the armchair. Mrs Talland herself had her blouse half off and for support was clinging to the sideboard.

"Who's that?" she had yelled at Julia's knock. "Is that you, Sally? Come in, can't yer? Come in, you little bitch! My God, I'll give you something!"

But when Julia entered she gave a gasp of surprise and altered her tones.

"S-sorry, dearie. Sorry, ma'am. Thought it was that little devil of a daughter. Come in, come in. If you only knew the trouble that girl gives me, regular little bad one she be. Sit down, m'dear. Sit down."

Wrinkling her nose in disgust, Julia did so and attempted to explain, although she felt she might just as well have been speaking to a brick wall. She said that Sally had been unwell at work, and was now resting at her house.

"And so I thought," she went on, "that if you had no objection, Mrs Talland, she might stay with me for the night."

Even through her bemused state the fact of being consulted was flattering to the woman's vanity.

"Of course," she said, "it's all right to me, quite all right. Though why you should be bothered with the brat's beyond me. Still – s'your funeral, m'dear, your funeral. Not much use to me here, she aren't, not by a long chalk. Nothing but cheek from the little bitch from morn till night."

Julia breathed relief. "Well then, I won't trouble you any further. I felt it my duty to let you know."

"An' quite right," the woman said whiningly, "more than *she'd* bother to do – if you was to know what I put up with ever since poor Ebenezer went! An' always treated her proper, I have. Don't know what I've done t'deserve it, I'm sure."

She snivelled while Julia got to her feet and went to the door. Once outside she took a deep breath, thankful for the freshening salt air from the sea.

Walking through the spring dusk back to Crab Street, a plan on behalf of Sally began to form in her mind. It was clear to her that studio work was not good for her, but suppose – for the time being anyhow – until someone else could be found to fill La Roche's place, she took the girl into her own flat, let her spend certain hours working domestically while she herself went down to the school?

Sally, of course, was not the ideal person to leave in her home, but it would mean a new life for her, and the idea appealed to Julia. Before she reached 7a she had already decided to broach the matter in the morning.

Before she went to bed that night, Julia went to Sarah's

room where Sally lay asleep, her pale hair spread round her face on the pillow. In repose, the insolence and bravado gone, the girl looked younger, more innocent, and Julia felt a queer tug of the heart when she remembered Caroline. Really, they were absurdly alike, the long lashes and wild rose colouring, the perfectly carved features. She's more like Caroline than Caroline's own children, Julia thought. Odd, considering her background.

The next day she suggested the plan.

Sally didn't at first appear pleased. "But I'm no good at cooking," she said, "and I don't like housework, anyhow."

"You could try it, and it wouldn't be hard. You know, Sally, I should help you quite a lot, and I think we could get along together."

"But I like the studio," the girl said stubbornly.

"I'm afraid that's out of the question," Julia told her. "After what's happened I couldn't take the responsibility again. Anyway, we always change our models each term, so you wouldn't have been there much longer."

Eventually Sally agreed to the idea and that same afternoon Julia paid a second visit to Mrs Talland.

This time the girl's stepmother was more on the defensive. "But I don't know as how I can manage," she said truculently. "She's not much use, I agree, but then there's times when she can help with the washing and such like."

"I shall pay her a wage," Julia answered. "No doubt she'll give you a portion, especially if you – "

"She'd better," Mrs Talland broke in, "after all I done for her."

"Yes, of course. I'm sure that can be arranged. Her wages won't be high, of course, I can't afford it. Still – "

"Very well," Mrs Talland said, "if she wants to leave me in the lurch, that's it. Always ungrateful she was, and in one way I can't say I'll be sorry to let her go. But you tell her she's to come and see me every week with a bit in the pocket. After all, in a sense it's an obligation put on me by Ebenezer to see she comes to no harm."

"She won't come to any harm through *me*," Julia said grimly.

"Good. So that's that."

162

Sally was installed permanently at the flat the same day in the small dressing room leading out of Sarah's room. She'd objected at first to any of her wages going to Mrs Talland.

"It isn't fair," she'd told Julia. "Why should she have it? She's done nothing for me."

"You're under age," Julia told her, "and she might refuse to allow you to come if we didn't humour her. But it's not only that. I'll see that she does your washing for you. We've no room for washing here, and if it went to the laundry you'd have to pay."

So Sally grudgingly was satisfied, and the next morning commenced her duties with Julia. During the first week or two she made an effort, although Julia soon realised she'd spoken truly over not liking housework. However, she seemed comparatively content, and with good food and an even routine, her looks improved. She put on a little weight and was neater, cared more for her appearance under Julia's vigilant eye.

She's really a beauty, Julia thought frequently, watching her. The sooner she's married the better.

In those early days, Julia generally managed not to be away from the house too long. But one afternoon she was kept at the studio later than usual. When she returned she heard voices from the doorstep, and going in found Peter in conversation with Sally over some photographs he was showing her.

"Why, Peter," Julia cried, "I didn't expect you."

He flushed. "Thought I'd look in, Mrs Kerr. I had to see a chap in Port Todric, and just called on the chance. Glad I've not missed you."

"Yes, so am I." But Julia was faintly perturbed. He really should have known better than to gossip with Sally.

"Sally," she said, "I'm sure Mr Storm would like a cup of tea. You can get it quite quickly, can't you? On the little table —"

As slight annoyance crossed Sally's face, Peter said quickly, "Oh, no, you mustn't trouble. It's late, and I've got to get back." She could see that in some way he was discomfited.

"No," Julia insisted, "you must have a cup. Besides I want to hear the news." When Sally had disappeared she asked, "Have you heard from Sarah lately?"

"What a question. We each write every other day. Even the medal business doesn't stop her. By the way – these are the snaps I took when she was over last. I was just showing them to – to the girl."

"Sally, yes. So I noticed." There was a pause before Julia continued casually, "I expect you were surprised to see my new help."

"I was rather." After a moment he added, "She's lovely, isn't she?"

"Yes. She has looks. She worked as a model at the studio, then I brought her here to get her out of a scrape."

"I see."

He was rather quiet. So Julia continued, looking at the snaps, "Have you two decided when to get married yet?"

He shrugged his shoulders. "It's up to Sarah. Sometimes it seems she cares more for her old art than she does for me. She's terribly sort of remote – well, not that exactly – but elusive somehow, Mrs Kerr. You can't always get near to her. And then at other times – oh, I dunno. It's rotten all this waiting."

"Have patience," Julia said. "It probably won't be so long now. When she knows about the medal I expect she'll come to the point."

But after Peter had left she settled down and wrote to Sarah.

I know you'll let me know as soon as you learn the result of the competition, but in the meantime, darling, if you really care for Peter, do make him feel he matters. After all, he's very attractive. I'm sure there are many women who would be only too glad to console him, and if you don't want this – well! Just think over what I've said.

Julia expected a quick reply from Sarah, but she didn't get it. It was a fortnight before she heard, and the letter was cool, almost curt.

If Peter's in love with *me*, other women won't count. We trust each other so please leave us to work things out ourselves.

Feeling rebuffed, Julia determined in future to do just that. May passed into June, and she began to prepare for two events, Sarah's return, and Stephen's. In his last letter he had told her that he expected to be free towards the end of the month, and should be with her at the latest by the beginning of July. This news excited Julia, made her feel almost a girl again.

"Where he'll sleep I don't know," she said to Sally one morning. "When Sarah's married of course arrangements will be simpler. In the meantime, there's always the sitting-room divan."

Sally agreed, shrugging with sulky disinterest. Julia felt irritated.

"Oh, do cheer up," she said impatiently. "What's the matter with you? I wish you could smile a little sometimes. Is there anything wrong?"

Sally tossed her head. "Why should there be?"

"No reason at all. It's just more pleasant to have a friendly face around than that sulky scowl. Now, Sally, cheer up. There are things to do. Count those handkerchiefs, will you, for the laundry."

Sally did so, with compressed stubborn lips. Julia sighed. She was beginning to think that the girl would never entirely settle down. There was a resentment about her, something defensive and hostile, which nothing, it seemed, could break.

Still, I've done my best for her, Julia thought, and if she doesn't like it here she'll have to go.

But the decision was not left to Julia. A week later she returned from the studio to find a letter written in Sally's sprawling handwriting lying on the table.

Opening it, Julia read:

Dear Mrs Kerr,

I'm sorry to leave like this, but I couldn't stick the housework. I've gone with Mr La Roche to be his model in London. It's all right, Ma knows, so it won't do any good making a fuss. Thanks for your trouble.

Yours,
Sally Talland

165

Julia found that she wasn't really surprised. Something like this was what she'd half expected. She laughed a little ironically. It just showed the stupidity of trying to help people who had already made up their mind. But she was sorry it was La Roche. He'd do her no good. Indeed, for Sally, this would mean but the beginning of an inevitable end. The little idiot.

Julia saw Mrs Talland and found that what Sally had said was quite true.

"Why shouldn't she go then?" Mrs Talland said truculently. "Sally and I don't always hit it off, but being a servant's no good to anyone. And I don't like the way you talked against me, that I don't. And when she come and asked my consent, as Ebenezer would have wanted – well, I give it, and that's that. Do better for herself in London by a long chalk, and going to send me more than *your* paltry bit, *and* a pair of earrings – *he* said so, Mr Roche. Nice man he is, respectable and nice-spoken. So don't you go sayin' nothin' against him, neither."

Oh, well, thought Julia going away, that's the end of that.

But she was tired. I'm done with helping people, she decided. Maybe I've been conceited to think I could. After all, who's got the right to decide other people's lives? What business have I got to think I know best?

In the dusk she smiled to herself. She remembered her husband saying to her once, 'When you find you can't make life and people behave exactly as you choose, Julia, you'll have grown up.'

Well, it had taken nearly seventy years. And still, sometimes, she was the defiant Julia of twenty. She had not yet learned completely to let go, to hand over the reins. But for the first time she found herself wanting to. Was it then that the school had served its purpose, or that some other plan was working itself through her?

After all, why not? she thought, walking along. I should still have some years ahead of me, I have experience behind me, and my brain's as quick as it ever was. With a little more rest and relaxation I'm sure the spring of creativeness would waken in me again. Perhaps my own work lies still in the future, perhaps the time has come for me to be free?

Unconsciously, her head lifted and her step lightened. She

began to envisage what the days might hold for her with the responsibility of the children gone, and the school out of her hands. All her life – at the back of her love, her activities and obligations – this one thing had remained intact and unspoiled, waiting for the chance to flower: the restless creative streak which she had been born with, and which would be with her until she died. People passed, phases passed, even emotion after a time became quietened and at rest. But the independence and flame of her own spirit – this went on, seeking fulfilment and peace.

And at last, she thought, the chance has come. At last, if I arrange things properly, I shall be able to give myself fully for the first time to my own work.

But she did not even then realise how soon things were to work out.

The following week in a letter from Sarah she learned that the Darrant medal had been won by her granddaughter.

And so you see, Nan, everything's all right. Peter and I will probably be married in August, if you agree, and you do agree, don't you, Nan darling? Then he's going to have a studio built for me over the stables. And, oh, Nan, something else – what do you think? – Mr Blair wrote to me quite recently and wanted to know when we were getting married. He's going to give us a cheque, isn't it nice of him? And, darling, have you *got* to go on with the school? You seem to have such foul luck with tutors – of course, after I'm married I might be able to come over and help there say two mornings a week. I expect I could.

This, of course, would not answer, Julia knew that. No, something else had to be thought out for the school.

That afternoon she went for a walk along the cliffs towards Praille. The day was windless and quiet, with a shell-grey sky over a calm sea. In the distance the familiar shapes of the fishing boats were outlined hazily in the faint summer mist. To her left the hills rose to their ageless line, towering jaggedly above the ruined mine relics, Praille Quoit standing stark and primitive on the highest ridge. The air was sweet and pungent with the breath of young bracken, thrift and sea. She drew it deeply into her lungs, realising acutely how, for a long time, she had missed her walks. She panted a little as she climbed the steep incline leading towards Trevaskiss Head. Then she sat down on a rock to rest.

Slowly she felt a serenity encompassing her that she'd never completely experienced before. And as she sat watching the waves lap lazily round the rocks below, the solution to her life, the answer to the pattern which had been for so long working out, came to her. She knew what she had to do. It was adieu. The time had come to say goodbye to the school. It had served its purpose. Through Sarah, and Sarah's talent, the name of Stephen Kerr and all he stood for, would now be remembered and carried on, surviving beyond the whims and foibles of any clique or fashion in painting.

In founding the Stephen Kerr School, Stephen had indeed built something of integrity which had weathered difficulties and criticisms through the years; but through Caroline's daughter he had done more – established that vital spark, that flame which would burn freely on, unrestricted by the petty squabbling and rivalries of groups and minor talent. Seen from this angle it was all, now, so simple and easy. She would give up the studio at the end of the term in July, and if anyone liked to start there on a new basis, under a new name, it was up to them. But for her it was over. It had all worked out, and this, she knew, was what Stephen himself would have wished.

Presently she got up and made her way back towards Port Todric. A thin little wind had sprung up from the sea, and the mist blew in a dim veil over the cliffs and path. An old delight and love for this place which had seen so many of her joys and sorrows filled her being. A glow crept into her cheeks so that when she reached Crab Street once more her skin was fresh as a girl's.

Absurd, she thought, absurd to say that youth is the best time. This is as good as any – to have memories, and to be able to enjoy them, to be able, even at my age, to look forward to the future. Life, indeed, is miraculous.

And so, with the miracle in her eyes still, she came to 7a. Inside the door she stood still, and for a moment was speechless. On a chair in front of her there lay a seaman's cap, and coming towards her with his arms held out, his curly hair about his laughing face, was Stephen – young Stephen.

The next moment she was in his arms and he had lifted her small figure off the ground.

"I'm home, Nan," he cried, "home for good. Me and you, Nan, and this old sea."

Trembling, she lifted her head, released herself, and stood looking at him. Yes, he was just the same, nothing had spoiled him. And she knew that in him, too, all that was good went on. In Sarah burned genius, but this boy, her beloved, was of life itself. All lay there in his open face – the capacity to live and suffer, love and enjoy as freely and naturally as the winds chasing the light of sun and shadow round the Cornish headlands.

"Stephen," she said, "oh, Stephen."

Just for a moment her eyes were filled with tears. It was ridiculous, of course, but everything for a brief second was too much for her. She felt almost too happy to live. Then she became aware of Stephen saying, "Gosh, Nan, I'm jolly hungry. What about a cup of tea and a pasty – got any pasties?"

"I'll look," she said smiling. "We'll soon see what we've got."

And still with that warm glow upon her, she went to the pantry.

Jean Chapman

The Bellmakers

Forced to take on her pedlar grandfather's tally round and sell stockings to save her family from starvation, Leah Dexter is unprepared for the abuse and prejudice she encounters travelling alone on the new railway. And when she arrives at the village of Soston just as brothers Ben and Nat are reclaiming the cursed Monk's Bell, the superstitious local folk take her appearance as an evil omen.

When Ben intervenes to save her he wins Leah's everlasting gratitude and heart. But prejudice, superstition and the unbridled lust of the squire's son still threaten the proud and beautiful pedlar girl and those she loves...

Further titles available from Woman's Weekly Fiction

While every effort is made to keep prices low, it is sometimes necessary to increase prices at short notice. Mandarin Paperbacks reserves the right to show new retail prices on covers which may differ from those previously advertised in the text or elsewhere.

The prices shown below were correct at the time of going to press.

☐ 1 86056 000 8	**A Place in the Sun**	Nina Lambert	£1.99
☐ 1 86056 005 9	**The Bellmakers**	Jean Chapman	£1.99
☐ 1 86056 010 5	**The Bridge Between**	Mary Williams	£1.99
☐ 1 86056 015 6	**Promise of Summer**	Rose Boucheron	£1.99
☐ 1 86056 020 2	**Tallie's War**	Jan Webster	£1.99
☐ 1 86056 025 3	**Time Will Tell**	June Barraclough	£1.99
☐ 1 86056 021 0	**Lucky Star**	Betty Paul	£1.99
☐ 1 86056 055 5	**With This Ring**	Jean Saunders	£1.99
☐ 1 86056 065 2	**A Captain's Lady**	Jennifer Wray Bowie	£1.99
☐ 1 86056 060 1	**Lily's Daughter**	Diana Raymond	£1.99

All these books are available at your bookshop or newsagent, or can be ordered direct from the address below. Just tick the titles you want and fill in the form below.

Cash Sales Department, PO Box 5, Rushden, Northants NN10 6YX.
Fax: 0933 414000 : Phone 0933 414047.

Please send cheque, payable to 'Reed Book Services Ltd', or postal order for purchase price quoted and allow the following for postage and packing:

£1.00 for the first book: £1.50 for two books or more per order.

NAME (Block letters) ....

ADDRESS ....

.... Postcode.............................

☐ I enclose my remittance for £........................

☐ I wish to pay by Access/Visa Card Number ⬚⬚⬚⬚⬚⬚⬚⬚⬚⬚⬚⬚⬚⬚⬚⬚

Expiry Date ⬚⬚⬚⬚

☐ If you do not wish your name to be used by other carefully selected organisations for promotional purposes please tick this box.

Signature ....
Please quote our reference: 3 503 500 C

Orders are normally dispatched within five working days, but please allow up to twenty days for delivery.

Registered office: Michelin House, 81 Fulham Road, London SW3 5RB

Registered in England. No. 1974080